WILLIAM
SHAKESPEARE'S

THE **CLONE ARMY** ATTACKETH

STAR WARS

PART THE SECOND

WILLIAM SHAKESPEARE'S

THE **CLONE ARMY** ATTACKETH

STAR WARS®

PART THE SECOND

By Ian Doescher

INSPIRED BY THE WORK OF GEORGE LUCAS
AND WILLIAM SHAKESPEARE

QUIRK BOOKS
PHILADELPHIA

Library of Congress Cataloging in Publication Number: 2014953127

ISBN: 978-1-59474-807-3

Printed in the United States of America

Typeset in Sabon

Text by Ian Doescher
Illustrations by Nicolas Delort
Production management by John J. McGurk

Quirk Books
215 Church Street
Philadelphia, PA 19106
quirkbooks.com

10 9 8 7 6 5 4 3 2 1

TO HESTON HAVENS AND TO SARAH CRESWELL:

TWO JEDI KNIGHTS BEYOND THE GALAXY

WHOSE KIND AND LOVING HEARTS SHALL NE'ER BE CLONED

DRAMATIS PERSONAE

CHORUS
RUMOR

YODA, *a Jedi Master*
OBI-WAN KENOBI, *a Jedi Knight*
ANAKIN SKYWALKER, *his Jedi apprentice*
MACE WINDU *and* KI-ADI-MUNDI, *Jedi Masters*
JOCASTA NU, *keeper of the Jedi archives*
PADMÉ AMIDALA, *senator of Naboo*
CORDÉ *and* DORMÉ, *her handmaidens and decoys*
CAPTAIN TYPHO, *of Amidala's guard*
BAIL ORGANA *and* ASK AAK, *senators of the Republic*
QUEEN JAMILLIA *and* SIO BIBBLE, *queen and governor of Naboo*
R2-D2, C-3PO, *and* R4-P17, *droids*
SHMI SKYWALKER *and* CLIEGG LARS, *Anakin's mother and her husband*
OWEN LARS *and* BERU WHITESUN, *Shmi's stepson and his mate*
JAR JAR BINKS, *a Gungan clown*
CHANCELLOR PALPATINE/DARTH SIDIOUS, *a Sith Lord*
COUNT DOOKU/DARTH TYRANUS, *a Sith*
MAS AMEDDA *and* DAR WAC, *vice chancellor and aide*
TAUN WE *and* LAMA SU, *cloners of Kamino*
JANGO FETT *and* BOBA FETT, *a bounty hunter and his son*
ZAM WESELL, *an assassin*
ELAN SLEAZEBAGGANO, *a wretch*
DEXTER JETTSTER *and* WA-7, *a Coruscant merchant and his droid*
NUTE GUNRAY, *viceroy of the Trade Federation*
WAT TAMBOR, SHU MAI, *and* SAN HILL, *Separatist Alliance conspirators*
POGGLE THE LESSER, *archduke of Geonosis*
ACKLAY, NEXU, *and* REEK, *beasts of Geonosis*
WATTO, *a tradesman of Tatooine*

SENATORS, PILOTS, GUARDS, DROIDS, CREATURES,
MEMBERS OF THE JEDI ORDER, *and* JEDI YOUNGLINGS

PROLOGUE.

Outer space.

Enter CHORUS.

CHORUS   All hurly-burly goes the galaxy—
The Senate sees a time of harsh unrest.
For many thousand systems do decree
Intent to leave th'Republic's troubl'd nest.
This movement of the sep'ratists is led   5
By one Count Dooku, garb'd in mystery.
The Jedi Knights are press'd and thinly spread:
The peace they keep grows weaker by degree.
A vital vote the Senate doth pursue:
Shall they an army for th'Republic make?   10
Strong senator—Am'dala of Naboo—
To Coruscant makes way, this plan to break.
In time so long ago begins our play,
In clash-strewn galaxy far, far away.

[Exit.

ACT
I

SCENE 1.

A landing platform on the planet Coruscant.

Enter PADMÉ, *in Naboo fighter ship, with* R2-D2.

PADMÉ   In sooth, I know not why I am so sad;
               Is this one moment not without its hope?
               The Senate doth face challenges, indeed,
               Yet need my visage sing such somber tones?
               The music of our strong democracy   5
               Hath instruments enough to keep its tune:
               A symphony of peace it hath perform'd,
               For many years delighting all who hear.
               The past, though, doth not croon the future's song.
               The minstrel of the present plays his lute   10
               As though to prophesy some tragedy
               And turn our joyful march to mournful dirge.
               E'en now there comes a frightful dissonance,
               A clang, a crash—the cymbals roughly struck.
               Our major calm, our time of quietude,   15
               Doth modulate unto a minor key.
               Too hastily we turn to drum and fife,
               The sounds of war assaulting ev'ry ear.
               My sadness, then, plays countermelody
               To these stark notes of conflict, pain, and strife. 20

Enter CORDÉ *dressed as* SENATOR AMIDALA *and* NABOO GUARDS,
in royal cruiser ship. Enter CAPTAIN TYPHO, *aside in fighter ship.*

GUARD 1	My senator, I bring this brief report:
	To Coruscant we make our swift approach.
CORDÉ	'Tis well, Lieutenant. Let us, then, proceed.
	Our royal cruiser shall its landing make,
	Beside the fighter ships escorting us. 25

[The Naboo royal cruiser and
fighter ships land on Coruscant.

R2-D2	Beep, meep, beep, whistle, squeak!
TYPHO	[*to Padmé:*] —We have arriv'd,
	And all within our party quite unscath'd.
	Forsooth, my trepidation was misplac'd:
	There was no cause or reason to have fear,
	No danger hath pursu'd us to this place. 30
	My guess was wrong, and we are landed safe.

[The royal cruiser explodes. Naboo guards die.

              Alas! How like a fool my spirits change—
              Methought I had been wrong, and now am wrong'd!

PADMÉ   [to Cordé:] O, Cordé, thou who took my rightful place,
              Unrightfully art slain through villainy.

CORDÉ   My lady, I have fail'd you in this death,
              And with my final breath beg you: forgive.
              I would I had another life to give,
              That you another death might still be spar'd.

                                     [Cordé dies.

PADMÉ   Weep, eyes, for sorrow comes too suddenly!

TYPHO   Good lady, you are yet in danger here.
              We must get hence and get you from this place.

PADMÉ   'Tis certain I should never have return'd.

TYPHO   Yet is this vote a thing of consequence,
              Which you and your estate may not dismiss.
              Young Cordé hath fulfill'd her duty true,
              If you would honor her, fulfill yours, too.

                                       [Exeunt.

SCENE 2.

On the planet Coruscant, in the chambers of the chancellor.

Enter CHANCELLOR PALPATINE, YODA, MACE WINDU, KI-ADI-MUNDI
      and other MEMBERS OF THE JEDI COUNCIL.

PALPATINE   The vote shall not suspended be for long;
              Star systems plentiful continue their
              Most swift departure to the sep'ratists.
              Thus doth the Senate presently demand
              A vote that shall decide if we shall see

An army in the strong Republic's name.

MACE   If they would in my country not remain—

PALPATINE   I shall not let the great Republic, which
              Hath stood for lo these thousand years as one,
              Be split in twain by any errant group,   10
              No matter how misguided they may be.
              Pray, trust me: my negotiations shall
              Not fail to bring those systems to our fold.

MACE   Yet if they fail, 'twould be the kiss of death:
              And we have not the Jedi to maintain   15
              The order and defense Republic needs
              Against a foe formidable as they.
              You would do well to bear this in your thoughts:
              We are but peacekeepers—not soldiers, nay.

PALPATINE   Wise Master Yoda, what do you foresee?   20
              Shall this grim path but lead to bitter war?
              Are all our steps directed thereunto?

YODA   The dark side rises—
              Cloudeth ev'rything it doth.
              Thus, the future hides.   25

Enter DAR WAC *in beam.*

DAR   Mahala, geena beeska wooski woo.

PALPATINE   The loyalists have come? My thanks, Dar Wac.

DAR   Ma hanna hoonja parawa.

PALPATINE   —Thou mayst
              Admit them to our presence even now.

                          [*Exit Dar Wac from beam.*

              Another time this matter we'll discuss,   30
              Yet now the delegation from Naboo

I must with all good will and comfort greet.

Enter PADMÉ, CAPTAIN TYPHO, BAIL ORGANA, JAR JAR BINKS,
and other NABOO GUARDS.

YODA   [*to Padmé:*] My dear Senator,
      Your tragedy whilst landing
      Most terrible was.   3

      Yet that you still live
      Bringeth feelings of deep warmth
      To this Jedi heart.

PADMÉ   My thanks, good Master Yoda. Do you have
      Suggestion as to who made this attack? 4
      Can your keen Jedi sight see e'en thus far?

MACE   Our best reports point to the twisted minds
      Of various spice miners who are found
      Upon the moons of your small home, Naboo.

PADMÉ   Nay, these reports have not the air of truth, 4
      For 'tis my sense Count Dooku is to blame.

KI-ADI   A shrewd political idealist is
      The man; to murther hath he not yet turn'd.

MACE   You know, my lady, Jedi was he once—
      'Tis true he's none in the new age, yet still 5
      His nature runs not to assassination.
      'Tis not within Count Dooku's character:
      The role of murderer he playeth not.

YODA   Yet most certain 'tis,
      Senator Amidala: 5
      In danger you are.

PALPATINE Brave Master Jedi, humbly I suggest
      The senator be safeguarded by you.

BAIL	Is't wise to play our hand in such a way,
	Since this grave moment bringeth such distress? 60
PADMÉ	Sir Chancellor, if you would hear me speak:
	'Tis not my wish, nor is it my belief—
PALPATINE	'Tis not your firm belief, young senator,
	Our situation hath become so dire?
	It may not be, and yet I disagree: 65
	The tide of these affairs hath turn'd most rough,
	And threatens now to overturn the ship
	Of our Republic. 'Tis most serious.
	Whilst I do grasp that this additional
	Security may be most noisome, it 70
	Is also vital you protected are.
	Mayhap if 'twere a Jedi you know well—

              A friend of times gone by, I have the man:
              E'en Master Obi-Wan Kenobi. Yea?

MACE   'Tis possible. He hath return'd e'en now: 75
              A border quarrel nearby Ansion—
              With each combatant raging like a moose—
              He hath of late o'erseen, and presently
              He hath made his return to Coruscant.

PALPATINE   If not for your fond people of Naboo,   80
              If not for the Republic that you serve,
              If not for this grim danger you are in,
              Do it, if not for these, then for my sake.
              When my mind ponders thought of losing you,
              'Tis more, my lady, than my soul can bear.   85

MACE   Brave Obi-Wan shall make report to you
              Immediately, lady. And, fear not:
              He shall be most discreet, and out of sight
              E'en though he ever guards you steadily.

PADMÉ   Kind Master Windu, take mine utmost thanks.   90
              [Exeunt Palpatine, Padmé, Typho, Yoda, Mace Windu,
                      Ki-Adi-Mundi, and Jedi Council members.

                 Enter ANAKIN SKYWALKER.

ANAKIN   Hold still, mine hands, be still, O fev'rish blood,
              If the mere thought of her doth move me so,
              How shall it be when I stand by her side?
              How when her lovely face doth meet mine eyes?
              What shall I do when mine ears hear her voice,   95
              Which is a sweeter music to my soul
              Above all else the galaxy could sound?
              The measure of my keen affection doth

Exceed all measure, line, or boundary.
And this affection, bred of memory,   100
Is but a shadow to what may come forth
When in her presence I shall stand at last.

Enter OBI-WAN KENOBI.

OBI-WAN   Good morrow, my young Padawan. How is't?
               What trouble's this in thy complexion here,
               What matter pulls thy spirit out of sorts?   105
ANAKIN   [*aside:*] Alas, how well he knows mine ev'ry look.
               [*To Obi-Wan:*] Nay, nay, 'tis nothing, Master. All
                                                          is well.
OBI-WAN   I sense the falsehood e'en as it is spoke—
               Thou art far tenser now than I have seen
               Since we into that nest of gundarks fell.   110
ANAKIN   A fallen memory indeed, kind sir,
               For it was you who did the falling whilst
               I did the rescuing, if I recall.
OBI-WAN   Perchance some fault befalls my memory—
               Forsooth, 'twas as thou sayest, I confess.   115
               Although 'twas frightening, it brings me mirth:
               Aye, danger may be merry when 'tis past.
               But now, behold thy face—thou dost perspire!
               I prithee, Anakin, relax, breathe deep.
ANAKIN   I have not seen the lass lo these ten years.   120
OBI-WAN   [*aside:*] I guess'd 'twas thoughts of Padmé plagu'd
                                                          him so.

Enter JAR JAR BINKS.

JAR JAR   'Tis Obi! Meesa smile to see you.
OBI-WAN   And thee as well, kind Jar Jar. Art thou well?

                    Enter PADMÉ *and* CAPTAIN TYPHO.

JAR JAR   O, Missa Padmé mees got palos!
             See, Senator, de Jedi commee.   12
PADMÉ   [*aside:*] Who is this man who stands before me here?
             There's Obi-Wan, I know him well enough,
             And is this—can it be? 'Tis Anakin.
             How unfamiliar is his face to me,
             How like a man and not the boy I knew!   13
             Though I feel I have ag'd but little since
             I last did see him, back on small Naboo,
             The change in him doth tell of many years
             That evidently fill'd the interim.
OBI-WAN   It is a joy to see you once again.   1
PADMÉ   It hath been years too many, Obi-Wan—
             Time's march continues on as quicksilver.
             And Ani? Is it thee? How thou hast grown!
ANAKIN   And thou as well, in charm and loveliness.
             I mean but loveliness most politic,   14
             And charm that doth befit a senator.
             'Twas nothing more I meant, nay, nothing more.
OBI-WAN   [*aside:*] How like a child he stammers, nervous wretch.
PADMÉ   O, Ani, whether I have grown or no,
             Thou shalt forever in mine eyes be that   14
             Small boy I met on windblown Tatooine.
OBI-WAN   Our presence here shall be invisible:
             This is my promise to you, Senator.

TYPHO   My name is Captain Typho, I provide
            Security unto Her Majesty.   150
            Our queen, Jamillia, hath been notified
            Of your assignment to the senator.
            Your presence here doth make me grateful, sir;
            The danger we are in, I'll warrant, is
            Far more than our dear senator admits.   15[5]

PADMÉ   'Tis not security I need, but answers,
            For guards I have enough, with questions more:
            Who is't who tried to kill me on the ship?
            And wherefore would they seek to harm me so?
            Is our Republic come to such a state?   16[0]

OBI-WAN   Our charge is to protect you, Senator.
            Investigation is not our command.

ANAKIN   We will discover who hath made assault
            Upon thy life, my lady: so swear I.

OBI-WAN   Our mandate shall not be exceeded, nay,   16[5]
            Speak thou not out of turn, my Padawan.

ANAKIN   I meant but in the interest of her
            Protection, Master, nothing more indeed.

OBI-WAN   I need not tell thee once again that thou
            Shouldst follow on my lead, young Anakin.   17[0]

ANAKIN   But wherefore?

OBI-WAN   —Eh? What didst thou to me say?

ANAKIN   Good Master, wherefore would they put us in
            Her service were it not to find the one
            Who was her vicious would-be murderer?
            Protection is a task fit for some brute,   17[5]
            A local force to keep a person safe,
            Requiring not a Jedi's skillful art.
            'Tis far beyond all reason to employ

         A Jedi in a simple sheriff's trade.

         In short: investigation is implied   180

         Within the prime directive we were giv'n.

OBI-WAN   We shall proceed exactly in the terms

         The Council hath instructed us, no more.

         We are not led by implication, lad.

PADMÉ   [*aside:*] This conversation is not for mine ears: 185

         The Jedi do forget themselves, I fear.

OBI-WAN   And thou shalt learn thy proper place, young one.

PADMÉ   Belike your presence shall reveal to us

         The mystery of whence the threat hath come.

         I prithee now, excuse me. I'll retire,   190

         For all shall be improv'd by rest and sleep.

                                [Exit Padmé.

TYPHO   I am reliev'd to have you here, good sirs.

         For my part, I shall station officers

         At ev'ry door, and take myself unto

         The center of control to watch o'er her.   195

               [Exeunt Obi-Wan and Captain Typho.

JAR JAR   Mees bustin' happy t'see you, Ani.

ANAKIN   She hardly recognized me, Jar Jar. Fie!

         Yet ev'ry day since we last met she hath

         Been forefront in my thoughts, the leading light

         Of ev'ry day that pass'd, surpassing all.   200

         She thought of me but little, if at all,

         I am a memory to her, forgotten.

         What foolishness I must have shown to her—

         My words fell trippingly from out my lips

         As though I were a simple-minded fool.   205

         Then Obi-Wan corrected me as though

         I were an errant child. So must I seem

To her, and him, and all of them besides.

Enter OBI-WAN KENOBI.

JAR JAR   But she's mo happy den in long time.
OBI-WAN   Thou art too focus'd on the negative.   210
                 Be mindful, Anakin, of all thy thoughts.
                 She was, indeed, most pleas'd to see us both.
                 I prithee, let us verify that all
                 The needed measures are in place to keep
                 The senator safeguarded and secure.   215
                               [*Exeunt Obi-Wan and Anakin.*
JAR JAR   Young Anakin would not speak with such ease—
                 Would not pour out the contents of his heart,
                 Would not with such a carefree boldness tell
                 The sorrows and complaints within his soul—
                 If he suspected I were more than fool.   220
                 For years I've watched among the senators,
                 The politicians' greed, the laws' delays,
                 The insolence of office, and the pow'r
                 That makes our little galaxy progress.
                 Is it a wonder turmoil comes to us,   225
                 Since we are led by such brutality?
                 Yet I may not my feelings true express:
                 I shall do what I may to set things right,
                 But never shall my fool's comportment fall.
                 I chose, aye, long ago, to play this role   230
                 And I shall play the part unto the end.
                 What would they say if Jar Jar suddenly
                 Spoke as they do, or show'd an aspect wise?
                 Why, they would think me mad e'en as I spoke
                 More sanely than I ever did before.   235

Nay, it shall not be so: I'll not remove
The mask I have put on. 'Tis for their sake:
For like this Anakin they comfort find
In having one among them simpler than
They know themselves to be. 'Tis passing strange.   240
These humans are a mystery to me,
E'en though I see them with an eagle's eye.
Thus, keep thy fervent peace now, Jar Jar Binks.
Forever may they think my mind is weak;
This giveth me th'advantage that I seek.   245

                                        [Exit.

SCENE 3.

On the planet Coruscant, in Padmé's chamber and on the city streets.

Enter RUMOR.

RUMOR   Into swift Rumor's net these mortals fly,
              Ne'er guessing that the traitor's there, within.
              Thus doth the cord of Rumor neatly tie
              Round all of them a band to wrap them in.
              O, see how I my merry pranks do play,   5
              Distracting them with votes and sep'ratists,
              Unknowingly they scramble on their way,
              Confus'd by fear that in their souls persists.
              Into this time of doubt, another comes
              Now entering the scene, a larger threat—   10
              Gainsaying the Republic in vast sums,
              Join'd with their enemies is Jango Fett.
              A vicious man and cruel to all his foes,

Ne'er was a bounty hunter so revil'd.
Giv'n to misanthropy, he hatred knows   1.
Of ev'ryone—except a twinlike child.
Full many whispers doth this Rumor spread,
Engaging ev'ry mind in fear and doubt.
To ev'ry ear doth come my voice of dread,
Till all the galaxy in pain shall shout.   2

                                     [Exit Rumor.

Enter JANGO FETT *and* ZAM WESELL *on balcony.*

ZAM   I hit the ship, sir, yet the job's not done:
             They did employ a decoy who's now dead,
             Yet our main target slipp'd away unscath'd.

JANGO   Yea, now we shall a stronger method employ.
             My client groweth ever more impatient, Zam.   2
             Pray, take thou this canister and let caution guide
             thine ev'ry step. Little though these beasts may be,
             they are most vicious—aye, and poisonous as well.
             E'en now go hence, and pray remember—I'll have
             no more mistakes, upon thy life.   3

                                       [Exeunt.

Enter OBI-WAN KENOBI *and* ANAKIN SKYWALKER.
Enter R2-D2 *aside, next to* PADMÉ, *who is asleep.*

OBI-WAN   Keen Captain Typho hath more men downstairs
             To guard the senator than we shall need—
             No smart assassin would make entrance there.
             Hast thou seen aught of substance?

ANAKIN   —Nothing, nay.
             'Tis quiet as an ancient ruin where   3

The dead lie still, unmoving in their tombs.
This waiting doth my better instincts thwart—
I would not on an incident attend,
Yet rather would preemptive action take.

[A sensor begins beeping.

OBI-WAN   What is't?

ANAKIN   —The cameras she cover'd o'er.   40
'Tis possible she did not like mine eyes
A'wand'ring o'er her as she tried to sleep.

OBI-WAN   But this is madness! What is in her mind?

ANAKIN   'Tis well—she set R2 to sound a loud
Alarum should a base intruder enter.   45

OBI-WAN   There are more ways than one a senator
To murther—R2 shall but warning make.

ANAKIN   'Tis true, and yet we would the killer catch.

OBI-WAN   Then hast thou plann'd to use her as thy bait?

ANAKIN   Accuse me not, I pray—'twas her idea.   50
No harm shall come to her, for with the Force
I sense whate'er befalls within that room.
The air could not shift in the least degree
But I would feel an 'twere a hurricane.
I bid you, trust me.

OBI-WAN   —'Tis a risk unwise.   55
Thy senses are not well enough attun'd,
Particularly where she is concern'd,
My young apprentice.

ANAKIN   —Yours are better, eh?

OBI-WAN   'Tis possible. Pray, set aside thy pride.

Enter ZAM WESELL *on balcony with* PROBE DROID.

ZAM   Go, droid, take thou these beasts and do my work   60

Of death and murther—aye, get hence! This night
Shall see my just reward for task completed.
Thus shall a senator a coffin fill,
And thus shall Jango Fett my coffer fill.

[*Exit Zam.*

PROBE   A trick, a trap, a sudden death,   65
Someone shall soon be out of breath!
When I drop off these kouhun bugs
They'll slink past curtains, walls, and rugs,
Delivering their lethal bite
Which shall bring death into the night.   70
'Tis bugs shall be the end of her—
We're off to kill a senator!

[*The probe droid flies to where Padmé sleeps.*

OBI-WAN   Thou lookest sore fatigu'd, young Padawan,
And should find sleep, not watch o'er one who doth.

ANAKIN   I do confess, I sleep not well of late.   75

OBI-WAN   Is it thy gentle mother, Anakin?

ANAKIN   Yea; she is ever subject of my dreams,
Though wherefore this should be, I do not know.

OBI-WAN   Dreams, like a storm, may pass in their own time,
Till all is calm and quiet once again.   80

ANAKIN   Much rather would I dreams of Padmé have,
Such storms I could endure eternally.
To be near her again begins a squall
Which riseth in my heart, as windstorm ne'er
Did blow upon the dunes of Tatooine.   85

OBI-WAN   Be mindful of these thoughts tempestuous,
They do betray a spirit blustery.
A Jedi does not row by waters rough,
But seeks calm waters and a steady sail.

Thy charts are fix'd: the Jedi order is   90
Thy destination and thy harbor true.
To change thy course would be most difficult.
And Padmé's but a politician sly,
Whose rudder may on any tide be mov'd.

                    [*The probe droid begins to cut*
                         through Padmé's window.

ANAKIN   Nay, she is unlike all the others in   95
          The Senate: even-keel'd, direct, and firm.
          Her glance could make a hundred storms be still,
          Her face could set a thousand ships aright.

OBI-WAN   In my experience, when politics
          Are at the helm, no course is ever true.   100
          These senators may seek to please those who
          Would fund campaigns and make them seaworthy,
          But nothing more. They'd cut the anchor of
          Democracy at tempest's first raindrop
          Without a thought, if they but funded are.   105

ANAKIN   Now shall I hear another lecture from
          The ancient mariner, e'en Obi-Wan.
          What do you know of economics, sir,
          Which rough, high seas were once your albatross?

                    [*The probe droid releases two kouhun*
                         bugs into Padmé's chamber.

PROBE   The merriment begins at once!   110
          The unsuspecting Jedi dunce
          Hath miss'd mine entrance to her room
          And shall, anon, behold her doom!

R2-D2   Beep, squeak! [*Aside:*] My scanner hath detected life,
          So shall I scan the chamber thoroughly.   115
          Nay, nothing by my scope discover'd is,

So shall I to my droidly sleep return.

               [The kouhun bugs crawl, advancing,
                             under Padmé's bedclothes.

PROBE   The droid hath miss'd them—pretties, go,

Be neither legs nor bodies slow!

With puncture swift our payment take,   12

And from this sleep she shall not wake.

ANAKIN   You do but draw a picture general,

Not ev'ry ship that sails th'Republic's seas

Is bound for stormy weather—Palpatine,

Let him stand for a counter to your point,   12

A bulwark 'gainst the flood of sep'ratists,

Our chancellor doth float a level tack.

OBI-WAN   'Tis Palpatine shall be thy paragon?

The man is politician through and through,

And is a clever navigator of   13

The passions and desires of senators.

            [The kouhun bugs prepare to strike Padmé.

ANAKIN   Yet I believe he is a noble soul,

Fit to direct our vessel—wait, alack!

OBI-WAN   I sense it, too—her room, let's thither go!

        [Obi-Wan and Anakin enter Padmé's room. Anakin
            brandishes his lightsaber, destroying the bugs.

PROBE   Our errand fails, and I must fly,   13

Be off into the darken'd sky!

If they should catch me stalking here

My master's punishment I fear.

             [Obi-Wan jumps through the window,
                 catching the probe droid.

PADMÉ   What's this—what hath occurr'd?

ANAKIN   —Stay here, I pray!

For Obi-Wan was right: a storm doth brew.   140

R2-D2   [*aside:*] O, curse my wires, I was not fast enough,
And now these gallant Jedi danger face!

> [*Exeunt Padmé and R2-D2. Exit Anakin severally.*
> *Obi-Wan continues to cling to the probe droid.*

OBI-WAN   Methinks this droid shall be the end of me,
For up and down Coruscant's busy lanes
It pulls me, with a mind to shake me loose.   145

Enter ANAKIN SKYWALKER *on balcony, climbing into a speeder.*

ANAKIN   On speeder's wings I fly most speedily,
My master to recover and protect
And rescue him from peril dire. E'en more,
I'll find the worthless rogue who doth attempt
To murther my most precious Padmé. Go!   150

> [*Exit Anakin in speeder.*

OBI-WAN   Past speeders several I barely dodge,
And see the fear on ev'ry driver's face.
They little do expect to see a man
A'hanging from a droid midst traffic jamm'd.
If I should fall, they may find bits of me   155
Strewn yon and hither on the city streets.
One driver calls me "Jedi poodoo"! Aye—
If I should fall upon the ground below,
His bitter prophecy may be fulfill'd:
I shall, like poodoo, make the bottom foul.   160

Enter ZAM WESELL *on balcony.*

ZAM   The droid returns, but what hangs thereupon?

           A Jedi Knight? Alas, I am undone—
           Some failure doth his presence here portend.
           Yet he shall not discover who I am,
           For he shall taste the ghastly consequence   165
           Of mine exacting rifle's fiery blast.

PROBE   O, thither stands my master, joy—
           This hanger-on doth so annoy!
           Yet what is that within her hand?
           Her rifle? I don't under—   170

                   [Zam shoots the probe droid,
                   destroying it, and Obi-Wan falls.

ZAM   'Tis done. Now I shall flee from wrath of Fett.
                             [Exit Zam.

OBI-WAN   From bad to worse this moment swiftly goes;
           All downward fly my chances to survive.
           Look how the ground doth speed toward my body—
           Let this not be the end of Obi-Wan!   175

           Enter ANAKIN SKYWALKER *in speeder.*

ANAKIN   Behold, I see him, falling yet alive—
           'Tis not the fall, but landing, that shall hurt.
           Now quickly, Anakin, fly just below,
           And give him space to break his fall with ease.
                  [Obi-Wan lands inside the speeder.

OBI-WAN   What kept thee? Hadst thou some employment
                               elsewhere?   180

ANAKIN   'Tis ever so when fac'd with such a choice—
           What speeder should I use? A cockpit must
           Be open to the air, with speed to match.
           The color must be pleasant to the eye.

A young man must consider this, so to   185
Bedeck himself with style, is this not true?

OBI-WAN   An 'twere thy skill with lightsaber were half
As sharp as thy most rapierlike wit,
Thou wouldst do well, e'en challenge Yoda's art.

ANAKIN   Methinks my skill doth match his even now.   190

OBI-WAN   Nay, only in thy mind, apprentice young.
Yet truly, hear my words: thou hast my thanks
E'en if I do not share thy jests. Indeed,
Thine humor I might find more humorous
Had not another fate befallen me.   195

ANAKIN   Befallen, verily, but less than fell.
You are alive—a blessing to us both—
And now let us pursue this villainy.

Enter ZAM WESELL, *flying in a speeder.*
OBI-WAN *and* ANAKIN *pursue her.*

OBI-WAN   He flieth straight below, into a dive.
Take care when thou dost follow, lest we crash—   200

Thou knowest well thou mak'st me sore afraid.

ANAKIN   I had forgot you liketh not to fly.

OBI-WAN   'Tis not the flying, 'tis the suicide—

I would not make a death by accident.

See now, the knave hath struck the power coupling!   205

Nay, drive not through its beam, thou pilot wild.

[Anakin navigates the speeder through
the power coupling's beams.

ZAM   His skill at navigation is most sure,

Yet I'll prevail and 'scape his keen pursuit.

[Zam flies into a tunnel.
Anakin continues by a different path.

OBI-WAN   What hast thou done—he flew another way!

ANAKIN   Good Master, prithee listen to my plan: 210

This chase shall but result in his demise

Within a sharp, untimely, fiery end.

I would prefer to question him, and to

Discover wherefore he hath tried to kill

And who hath sent him here upon this chore.   215

I have employ'd a shorter path, methinks,

Which shall deliver him to us anon.

OBI-WAN   Yet where is he? It seems he hath been lost.

'Twas shorter, aye, for now we are made short:

Short of the villain we did hotly seek,   220

Who did fly by a pathway opposite.

Again, thou provest only that thou art—

ANAKIN   I bid thee, sir, excuse me. I must fly!

[Anakin jumps from the speeder in pursuit
of Zam, who reappears below.

OBI-WAN   That rascal, he doth ever swagger so.

[Exit Obi-Wan.

ANAKIN   E'en with the traffic circling all around   225
                 'Tis quieter sans Obi-Wan's harangues.
                 I spy him now, and on his speeder land!
                 The rogue is mine, and soon shall he be stopp'd.

ZAM   What is this, can it be? He boardeth me!
                 We shall yet see if he can keep his grip   230
                 When I do jostle him both here and there.
                 Mayhap I'll ram him on a strong blockade,
                 Or let him feel another speeder's thrust.

ANAKIN   I see the beast, and 'tis not he, but she!
                 If I have seen aright, in her distress   235
                 She chang'd her form. Our enemies may bring
                 Us trouble vast indeed, if they—like moons—
                 Are changeable. Now out, lightsaber, come:
                 Do thy swift work, unto the cockpit strike!
                 Yet she doth shoot at me, and from mine hand   240
                 Like captur'd bird my lightsaber doth fly.

ZAM   His weapon's gone, but still he doth hold fast.
                 What's this—he grasps mine hand, my blaster too,
                 We struggle—ah! Now all controls unto
                 My speeder are by laser's strike destroy'd!   245
                 My ship doth fall, and quickly comes the street.
                 Into the crowds of passersby we fall.
                 [Zam's speeder crashes onto the streets of Coruscant.

ANAKIN   I leap e'en now, my life thereby to keep.
                      [Anakin jumps from the speeder as it crashes.

ZAM   The speeder's down, but still my feet may fly.

ANAKIN   What, ho! Stop now, thou rogue, for thou art mine!   250
                      [Exit Zam into a nightclub.

Enter OBI-WAN KENOBI.

OBI-WAN	Say, Anakin! 'Tis well that we have met,
	For I did worry o'er thy safety. Now,
	How goes the chase? Hast seen the roguish knave?
ANAKIN	Just fled into this club of ill repute.
	Let us make entrance, bring the beast without. 25
OBI-WAN	I bid thee, patience, use the mighty Force.
	Call on thine instincts, not thy taste for blood.
ANAKIN	Apologies, my master.
OBI-WAN	—He went in
	To hide, and not to flee, or he'd be gone.
	Belike 'tis not from us that he would run. 26
	Behold, my Padawan, thy lightsaber,
	Which went a'flying past my head as thou
	Didst bravely fight the nasty criminal.
	I caught it barely as it pass'd me by.
	Mayhap in future battles thou shalt keep't? 26
	Remember, Anakin, this weapon may
	The diff'rence be between thy life or death.
ANAKIN	I shall endeavor to recall your words.
OBI-WAN	Why is't I feel thou shalt to me be death?
	In some yet unknown place, some lonely star, 27
	It may be that thou shalt, in future battle,
	Make some mistake within the episode
	That brings one death to me—or three or four.
ANAKIN	'Tis now your jests ring hollow on mine ears.
OBI-WAN	Our wits are misalign'd tonight, in troth. 27
ANAKIN	Speak not of some misfortune I would bring,
	For you, dear sir, are like the father that
	I ne'er did know, nor do, nor ever shall.
OBI-WAN	If this be so, wherefore attend me not?
ANAKIN	I try, my master, yet my youthful ears 28
	Have learn'd to tune to sounds beyond your voice.

They enter the nightclub. Enter ZAM WESELL, *hidden,*
and several CREATURES *at the bar.*

OBI-WAN   Dost thou see him herein?

ANAKIN   —Your "he" is "she,"
               And more than that, a changeling.

OBI-WAN   —Is it so?
               Then must we cautious be especially.
               I prithee, go and find her where she hides.   285

ANAKIN   I shall indeed. But, sir, where are you bound?

OBI-WAN   Unto the bar—my whistle there to wet.

ANAKIN   [*aside:*] 'Tis not the time to drink, but shrewdly think.
                              [*Exit Anakin. Obi-Wan approaches the bar.*

Enter ELAN SLEAZEBAGGANO.

ELAN   Greetings, sir, allow me your pleasure to ensure,
               for I've such wonders as shall act unto your soul as   290
               surgeon. My death sticks, perhaps, you would care
               to try—they are most belovèd by the population general.
               You shall intoxicated by, 'tis my promise and warning.
                              [*Obi-Wan uses a Jedi mind trick on Elan.*

OBI-WAN   Thou dost not wish to sell death sticks to me.

ELAN   I'd not sell you these death sticks. Nay, not I.   295

OBI-WAN   Thou shalt go home, and there rethink thy life.

ELAN   I must go thither to rethink my life!
                              [*Exit Elan.*

Enter ANAKIN SKYWALKER.

ANAKIN   Where is the scoundrel? I must find her out.
               Yet this dark club is so completely full

300

I could not find a bantha hiding here,
Much less an agile, shifty killer. Fie!

          [Zam approaches Obi-Wan from behind.

ZAM   These Jedi have pursu'd me here, but one
Hath turn'd his full attention to the bar,
There to assuage his thirst. Aye, drink your fill—
For it shall be the last thy lips shall taste.   305
Step closer now, whilst he doth lap his cup,
And soon shall he imbibe my blaster's fire.

        [Obi-Wan turns around quickly, cutting off
        Zam's hand with his lightsaber.

OBI-WAN   O, brutish fiend, thy villainy is done!
Let us go hence, and learn the total truth
Of thy most traitorous and awful deeds.   310

ANAKIN   *[to onlookers:]* Be ye at ease, this is a Jedi case.
Continue with your drinks—our mug is found.

        [Exeunt creatures as Obi-Wan, Anakin,
        and Zam exit to the street.

OBI-WAN   *[to Zam:]* Dost thou know who it was thou tried
        to kill?

ZAM   A senator, the one come from Naboo.

OBI-WAN   And who was it employ'd thee—speak thou true!   315

ZAM   'Twas but employment minor, nothing more.

    Enter JANGO FETT *on balcony.*

JANGO   *[aside:]* Mine operative hath been caught, they have
found Zam. If I do not act swiftly, shall not be she
that's found—it shall be I. Go to them, Zam, I'll find
another underling. Forsooth, e'en from this moment   320
I'll remember: if I will have a job done right, it shall
be done myself.

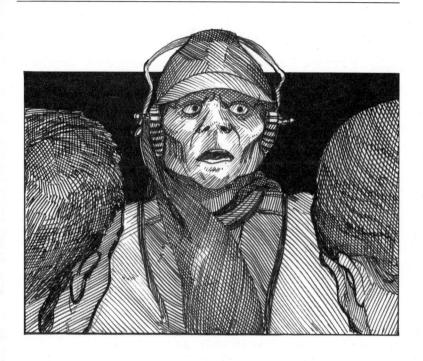

ANAKIN	I bid thee, tell us; all shall soon be well.	
	Aye, tell us now, else shalt thou feel my rage!	
ZAM	It was a brutal bounty hunter nam'd—	325
	[Jango Fett shoots Zam with a poisonous dart.	
	Weh shanit, sleemo—death is now my task.	
	[Zam dies. Exit Jango Fett.	
ANAKIN	Our questions are not answer'd, yet again!	
OBI-WAN	This toxic dart that made the killer's end	
	Brings yet another question, which, in time,	
	May lead to answers. Patience, Padawan.	330
	Let us return, and bring this news unto	
	The Jedi Council. They shall serve as guide—	
	Their wisdom shall be unto us supplied.	
	[Exeunt.	

SCENE 4.

On the planet Coruscant, the Jedi temple and the freighter docks.

Enter OBI-WAN KENOBI, ANAKIN SKYWALKER, YODA, MACE WINDU,
KI-ADI-MUNDI, *and other* MEMBERS OF THE JEDI COUNCIL.

YODA	These tidings ill are.
	Track down this bounty hunter
	You must, Obi-Wan.
MACE	This killer hath our back against the wall.
	Be sure you do discover who it is 5
	By whom the bounty hunter is employ'd.
OBI-WAN	And what of Amidala? She requires
	E'en more protection than she had before.
YODA	Your Padawan, yea—
	'Tis he shall escort her back, 10
	Unto Naboo's shores.
MACE	Young Anakin, take thou the senator,
	Return unto her planet, e'en Naboo.
	She shall be safer there, and furthermore:
	Do the right thing and use a transport that 15
	Is yet unregister'd. Thus may her foes
	Find all her movements difficult to track.
ANAKIN	Yet as the senator doth claim her place
	As leader of the opposition, it
	Shall be most difficult to give sound cause 20
	Why she must leave the capital anon.
	Belike she shall refuse. What then, I pray?
YODA	Until this killer
	Found hath been, our judgment true
	Respect she must, hmm. 25

MACE   Go thou unto the Senate, Anakin,
            There ask the chancellor, e'en Palpatine,
            To plead our cause herein; 'tis strictly bus'ness.
                    [Exeunt Yoda, Mace, Ki-Adi-Mundi, Obi-Wan,
                            and other Jedi Council members.

                    Enter CHANCELLOR PALPATINE.

ANAKIN   Wise Chancellor, you come in perfect time.
PALPATINE   Indeed?
ANAKIN   —The Jedi Council doth request   30
            Your keen assistance in a matter most
            Important to their cause and to my heart.
PALPATINE   Whate'er they ask, I do but live to serve.
ANAKIN   Would you speak to the lady senator,
            E'en Amidala of Naboo, and ask   35
            That she accept the Jedi's sage advice
            To make departure swift from Coruscant,
            Returning to her home on small Naboo?
PALPATINE   [*aside:*] What fools these Jedi be! [*To Anakin:*]
                                            Indeed I shall.
            The senator shall in no wise refuse   40
            Explicit order of th'executive.
            Her character I understand enough
            To give such reassurance unto thee.
ANAKIN   You have my gratitude, Your Excellence.
PALPATINE   Thus art thou finally assignment giv'n—   45
            Thy patience all this time earns its reward.
ANAKIN   It is your guidance, which you nobly pay
            To me, and have since I was but a boy,
            That brings reward, e'en more than patience mine.

PALPATINE   Thou hast no need of guidance, Anakin.
             In time, thy spirit shall make recompense
             For any credit I have proffer'd thee
             When thou hast learn'd to trust thy feelings true:
             Forsooth, then shalt thou be invincible.
             So have I laid my wager many times: 5
             Of all the Jedi I have ever seen,
             Thy treasure and thy skill exceed each one.
ANAKIN   Your words do humble me, Your Excellence.
PALPATINE   I have foreseen that thou shalt strong become,
             Dear Anakin, beyond the Council—aye,   6
             Beyond e'en Obi-Wan, Mace Windu, or,
             If I may say: e'en Master Yoda too.
                                                     [Exit Palpatine.
ANAKIN   How doth this man speak words that seem to burn!
             It is as though this Palpatine hath turn'd
             To dragon: clad with scales against a strike,   6
             Protecting him from ev'ry blast as though
             They were of iron forg'd in flames of blue,
             With forkèd tongue that traces ev'ry scent
             Of fear upon his hapless enemies,
             Such claws that are as sharp as blades of steel,   7
             Design'd for tearing or to puncture flesh—
             E'en to a person's soul these knives may grasp,
             A tail with which to sweep away his foes,
             Such strength within as could an army face,
             With broadest stroke may fell a mountaintop,   7
             Behold, such wings of iridescent hue,
             Equipping him to fly or flee at once,
             To make attack or make escape at will.
             Yet all these instruments of dragonhood

Are but the prologue to the savage fire   80
That scorcheth all when he doth ope his mouth!
Shall I the greatest Jedi ever be?
Is't possible that I may yet exceed
The skill of Obi-Wan, or Yoda, too?
How like a blaze the dragon's luring words   85
Do play their sparks and flashes on mine ears,
Do stoke the fierce inferno in mine heart.
Indeed, I would hear more of his hot speech,
For it doth warm my spirits through and through.
The dragon Palpatine doth fascinate: 90
He frightens and entices, both at once.
Yea, I admire his monster qualities
And would most gratefully be taught by him
How I may wake the dragon that's within.

[Exit Anakin.

Enter YODA, MACE WINDU, *and* OBI-WAN KENOBI
above, on balcony.

OBI-WAN   Concern'd I am for my young Padawan.   95
     He is not ready this assignment to
     Receive and undertake, not on his own.
YODA   The Council thinks not,
     And utmost confidence hath
     In its decision.   100
MACE   Incredible's the talent of the boy.
OBI-WAN   Yet, Master, still he doth have much to learn.
     'Tis true the boy hath vast abilities,
     But they have made him somewhat arrogant.
YODA   Indeed, Obi-Wan,   105

    A flaw growing common in
    The Jedi order.

    Too sure the Jedi,
    Too sure of wisdom, of skill,
    E'en the older ones.   110

MACE   I prithee, do remember, Obi-Wan:
    If it may be the prophecy is true,
    Then in the universe's smelting pot—
    Wherein our galaxy is bent and shap'd—
    Your young apprentice is the iron man   115
    Who shall forge balance in the Force again,
    And fix our cause as metal 'gainst the dark.
              [Exeunt Yoda, Mace, and Obi-Wan.

Enter ANAKIN SKYWALKER, PADMÉ, *and* JAR JAR BINKS.

PADMÉ   *[to Jar Jar:]* A leave of absence I must take anon,
    And thou must in the Senate take my place.
    Come, Jar Jar Binks, my representative: 120
    I know I may on thy good judgment trust.

JAR JAR   O, meesa pleas'd to take this burthen,
    Accept with muy humility.

PADMÉ   My thanks, kind Jar Jar. I'd not hold thee here—
    Well do I know the urgent nature of   125
    Thy vital new responsibilities.

JAR JAR   'Tis so, my lady. Now I goin'.
    [Aside:] And shall do what I may to work for right!
              [Exit Jar Jar.

PADMÉ   *[to Anakin:]* This Jedi plan, which is to hide in fear,
    Doth not conform unto my strong desire—   130

	To stay and show my strength, e'en 'gainst this threat.
ANAKIN	Fear not. The Council hath decreed that there

ANAKIN   To stay and show my strength, e'en 'gainst this threat.

Fear not. The Council hath decreed that there
Shall be a full investigation; it
Shall not be long e'er Master Obi-Wan
Hath caught the worthless bounty hunter who   135
Hath order'd this attack upon thy life.

PADMÉ Shall it be all for naught that I have work'd
This bygone year against the act that would
Create an army in Republic's name?
Are all mine efforts so in vain that I   140
May not be present when its fate is seal'd?
It is as though I run a vital race
And in the final moments have been forc'd
To wander off the track and forfeit all.
'Tis more than just unfair, aye, 'tis unjust!   145

ANAKIN At times we must our errant pride release
And do that which is ask'd of us instead.

PADMÉ Thy words do sting, yet show that thou hast grown.

ANAKIN My growth is still by Obi-Wan ignor'd.
Pray understand: the man's a mentor true,   150
With wisdom like to Master Yoda's wit,
With power like to Master Windu's strength.
'Tis fortunate I his apprentice am.
Yet hear me now, judge thou mine honest boast:
In many matters I exceed the man.   155
Prepar'd I am the trials for to face,
Yet he believes me unpredictable
And shall not let my Jedi rank advance.

PADMÉ Thou must in this a deep vexation find.

ANAKIN 'Tis worse than mere vexation. He gives more   160
Of criticism than I do deserve,

	He lends opinion freely, but doth not
	So willingly give ear to hear my words.
	In troth: the man doth understand me not.
	When I am thusly clipp'd, how may I grow? 16.
PADMÉ	Hath bud e'er blossom'd sans the watchfulness
	A gardener doth skillfully extend,
	E'en when 'tis time to wield the pruning shears?
	Our mentors see the worms, the quick decay,
	The stems that in the wrong direction sprout— 17(
	They pluck where 'tis most needed, such that flow'rs
	As we may bear our fragrance to the world.
ANAKIN	'Tis true, I know 'tis true—I have my weeds.
PADMÉ	So let thy beauty flourish in its time,
	And seek thou not to force untimely growth. 17:
ANAKIN	Yet I am fully grown, and would unfurl
	My petals to the wind—and to thy notice.
PADMÉ	Look not upon me with such seedy eyes.
ANAKIN	And wherefore not?
PADMÉ	—It drives my bud to rot.
ANAKIN	Apology I give thee, worthy rose, 18(
	For bringing such a stench unto thy nose.
	[*Aside:*] Thus have I planted root of love too soon.

Enter OBI-WAN KENOBI, CAPTAIN TYPHO, DORMÉ, *and* R2-D2.

TYPHO	Most worthy lady, time has come to leave.
	I pray, be safe until we meet again.
PADMÉ	Kind Captain Typho, thanks, and take thou care 18:
	Of Dormé, for the threat now falls to you.
DORMÉ	He shall be safe with me.
PADMÉ	—Whence come these tears?

	I'll warrant thou shalt be kept well secure.	
DORMÉ	'Tis not for me I weep—nay, 'tis for you,	
	And for the fear I feel for your own sake.	190
	What if your enemies discover you	
	Have fled the capital back to Naboo?	
PADMÉ	Then shall we see this Jedi prove his worth	
	And show the skill that shall protect my steps.	
OBI-WAN	Good Anakin, a word before thou goest:	195
	Do nothing sans the consultation of	
	The Jedi Council or myself. Dost hear?	
ANAKIN	It shall be so, my master.	
OBI-WAN	[to Padmé:] —Senator,	
	I shall unveil this vicious plot anon,	
	So shall you hither make return at once.	200
PADMÉ	I shall most grateful be for ev'ry speed	
	You may deliver, Master Obi-Wan.	
ANAKIN	We must away.	
PADMÉ	—I follow; lead thou on.	
OBI-WAN	The Force be always with thee, Anakin.	
ANAKIN	With you as well, good master mine. Adieu.	205
OBI-WAN	[to Typho:] I hope the boy shall nothing foolish try.	
TYPHO	'Tis she, not he, who makes me worry, though:	
	The young may work our older nerves some woe.	

            [Exeunt Obi-Wan, Captain Typho, and Dormé.

PADMÉ	Upon the moment shakes mine heart with fear.	
ANAKIN	My first assignment 'tis: I fear as well.	210
	All shall be well, R2 shall keep us safe.	
R2-D2	Beep squeak! [Aside:] He makes this comment as a jest,	
	Yet I shall offer them my very best.	

                                      [Exeunt.

ACT II

SCENE 1.

On the planet Coruscant, in Dex's Diner and the Jedi archives.

Enter Obi-Wan Kenobi, WA-7, *and assorted diners.*

WA-7   What ho, Dex, here's a man to speak with you—
              A Jedi, if his look doth not deceive.

              Enter Dexter Jettster.

DEXTER   By my six limbs, 'tis Obi-Wan Kenobi!
OBI-WAN   Good morrow, Dex, 'tis well to see thee!
DEXTER   —Yea!
              I prithee, sit thee down and rest awhile.
              I'll come within thy radius anon.
WA-7   Would you enjoy some Jawa juice, good soul?
OBI-WAN   Indeed, thou hast my thanks.
DEXTER   [*embracing him:*]   —My longtime friend!
              What knowledge may I arm thee with today?
OBI-WAN   I bid thee, Dex: pray tell, what's this device?   1
                     [*Obi-Wan shows Dexter the poisonous dart.*
DEXTER   Zounds! Such a thing! I've not seen one of these
              Since I did prospect on far Subterrel,
              At the extremity of th'Outer Rim.
                              [*WA-7 serves Obi-Wan his Jawa juice.*
OBI-WAN   And dost thou know, then, whence it comes? [*To WA-7:*]
                                                    My thanks.
DEXTER   This little thing, no more than pinkie's length,   1
              Belongs to cloners, they who live far off.
              'Tis known as a Kamino saberdart.
OBI-WAN   Yet when I put it to analysis,

	Our archives knew naught. Wherefore, wonder I?	
DEXTER	These cuts upon the side, these members here,	20
	Do tell the story of their genesis.	
	The droids that analyze such things but look	
	For symbols. Thus, they may not heed such grooves.	
	O, shame, good Obi-Wan! I would have thought	
	The Jedi would exhibit more respect	25
	Toward the difference that one may find	
	Twixt knowledge and its older sister: wisdom.	
OBI-WAN	Yea, yet if droids could think we'd all be lost,	
	Trapp'd in an abject matrix of machines.	
	But to the point: Kamino is a name	30
	With which I'm unfamiliar. Doth it lie	
	Within the fair Republic's boundaries?	
DEXTER	Nay, 'tis beyond the fingertips of our	
	Republic, far beyond the Outer Rim.	
	Belike twelve parsecs past the Rishi Maze.	35
	It should be simple to discover it,	
	E'en for those archive droids of thine, my friend.	
	Be wary, though, Kaminoans unto	

Their own do keep—their own that multiply,
For they are cloners, sharply skill'd to boot.   4

OBI-WAN   These cloners, are they like to act as friends?

DEXTER   That doth depend. If I could future tell,
Or read the meaning to be found in palms,
Thou'dst find this Dex not in this diner here.

OBI-WAN   Well do I know. But thou hast said "depend"—   4
Depend on what, thou jolly knave? Speak on.

DEXTER   On how thou dost comport thyself, good man,
On whether they do feel they've elbow room
To test the limits of thy pocketbook.

OBI-WAN   My thanks, dear friend, thou art a helping hand.   5

                    [Exeunt Dexter, WA-7, and restaurant patrons
                              as Obi-Wan leaves the diner.

A mystery's afoot, with clues but scant.
We Jedi are protectors, wise and true,
Sent forth to champion Republic's cause.
Detective work hath rarely been my call,
Yet now I find myself embroil'd in this   5
Most strange and enigmatic happening.
A poison'd dart, and hints of distant cloners:
These are the smatterings with which I must
Make sense of an obscure conspiracy.
The late attack upon the senator   6
Hath pointed to the bounty hunter fled.
The bounty hunter's instrument of death
Doth point toward Kamino, far remov'd.
This foreign planet, of which I know naught,
Points me unto the Jedi archives now.   6
Mayhap 'tis thither I shall answers find.

Enter JOCASTA NU, *as* OBI-WAN KENOBI *enters the Jedi archives.*

JOCASTA   Let me my full assistance proffer, sir.
OBI-WAN   Indeed, I'd be most grateful if thou wouldst.
JOCASTA   Belike, Master Kenobi, you are here
              Replete with questions dancing in your mind,   70
              A problem truly difficult to solve?
              Reveal it unto me; I'll give you aid.
OBI-WAN   In this thou speakest well, for I do seek
              A planetary system call'd Kamino.
              No system thus nam'd holds the archive charts.   75
              [Obi-Wan and Jocasta approach an archive computer.
JOCASTA   Such name I've never heard in all my years—
              Are you most sure of its coordinates?
              Review, I bid you, what you have been told.
OBI-WAN   Expected I the unknown planet should
              Appear within this quadrant—yea, e'en here—   80
              Which lieth just below the Rishi Maze.
JOCASTA   Except no system doth appear therein,
              So it doth not exist: it must be thus.
OBI-WAN   O, marry, 'tis impossible, methinks—
              Mayhap the archives are but incomplete.   85
JOCASTA   Existence hath it none declare the archives!
                                                 [Exit Jocasta.
OBI-WAN   The trail runs even colder, if indeed
              The system I most keenly seek doth hide.
              Perchance a wisdom far beyond mine own
              Can help uncover what I would reveal.   90
              Thus, onward, Obi-Wan, and Yoda seek—
              Mayhap his sage, calm intellect may find
              The answer to which I am thus far blind.
                                                 [Exit.

SCENE 2.

On the freighter to Naboo and on the planet Naboo.

Enter PADMÉ, ANAKIN SKYWALKER, R2-D2, A SERVING DROID,
and ASSORTED PASSENGERS.

DROID   [*to R2-D2:*] Go hence, thou brutish knave, we serve
                                        no droids!
                                    [*Exit serving droid.*

R2-D2   [*aside:*] Belike he would appreciate
               A serving of my fury on his pate.
               We droids are e'er revil'd, e'en by our own—
               Thus must I toil each hour to prove my worth   5
               And show the noble soul that lies within.
               [*To Padmé:*] Beep, whistle, meep.

PADMÉ   —Mine humble thanks, R2.
               [*To Anakin:*] What thinkest thou, is't difficult to hand
               Thy life entire unto the Jedi order?
               Thus mayst thou never visit where you like,   10
               Nor things thou dost enjoy engage withal.

ANAKIN   Indeed, or be with those I truly love.

PADMÉ   Yet doth the Jedi code allow for love?
               Methought that love was for the Jedi bann'd,
               Forbidden by the order. Is't not so?   15

ANAKIN   Attachment is prohibited, 'tis true.
               Possession is prohibited as well.
               Compassion, though—love unconditional—
               Is central to a Jedi's ev'ry step.
               Thus from a certain point of view it may   20
               Be said we are encourag'd to spread love.

PADMÉ   'Tis clear the words I spoke before did err,

The boy I knew those years ago is gone,
For thou hast chang'd so much in time's swift stride.

ANAKIN   Yet thou art constant as the rising sun: 25
Unchanging, faithful, bringing light to all.
Thou art as I bethink thee in my dreams.

PADMÉ   [*aside:*] Such dreams of me he doth with ease confess,
Which doth both shock and move my lonely heart.

ANAKIN   Behold, it is thine home, for we arrive   30
Upon the verdant shores of sweet Naboo.

    [Exeunt passengers as Padmé, Anakin, and R2-D2
              make their way to the court of Naboo.

PADMÉ   My mother country, land where I was born—
Each time I see her, I am all delight.

ANAKIN   Thou heardest of my dreams, my lady—tell
Me, what was it like to be queen of Naboo?   35

PADMÉ   Though I was very young, I was not yet
The youngest queen elected in Naboo.
Yet as I do look back, I wonder if
I was prepar'd the task to undertake.
Belike I was not old enough to bear   40
The onerous responsibility.

ANAKIN   And yet thy loyal people do believe
That thou didst serve them well. Did they not move
To so amend the law that thou couldst stay
A longer time as their belovèd queen?   45

PADMÉ   It was relief beyond all measure when
My double term was up and I was free.
When our new-minted queen did call on me
To serve the Senate, I could not refuse.

ANAKIN   Aye, she did judge aright, for sorely doth   50
Th'Republic need strong voices such as thine.

It pleaseth me that thou didst choose to serve,
As I work t'ward the fair Republic's good.

Enter QUEEN JAMILLIA, SIO BIBBLE, *and* MEMBERS OF
THE NABOO COURT.

PADMÉ   My queen, your humble servant hath arriv'd,
And swiftly shall I give you my report: 5
The vote is near and shall be ta'en anon.
I fear that if the senators do vote
To make an army in Republic's name,
We'll see a period of civil war.

SIO   It must not be! We've not seen war to such   6
Degree since our Republic first was form'd.

JAMILLIA   Do you see any way, good Senator,
That we through some negotiation may
Convince the sep'ratists to end this threat,
And join, once more, into th'Republic fold?   6

PADMÉ   If they feel threaten'd, they shall never join
The flock, but go astray like errant sheep.
They shall flee to the Commerce Guilds or to
Trade federations, which shall shepherd them.

SIO   This bleating must be stopp'd—outrageous 'tis!   7
Yet after trials four within the court
Supreme, Nute Gunray still doth wield his staff
As viceroy of the Federation. Fie!
I fear the Senate is too far afield,
All powerless this crisis to resolve.   7

JAMILLIA   We must, as lambs, look to the larger herd
And keep faith that our brave Republic shall
Know how to guide this situation right.

	The day when we are shorn of our belief	
	In strong democracy, upon that day	80
	It shall be lost to us eternally.	
PADMÉ	In all mine orisons I pray that day	
	May never come, your noble Majesty.	
JAMILLIA	Meanwhile your welfare here is paramount.	
SIO	Good Master Jedi, what can you suggest	85
	The senator's defense to guarantee?	
PADMÉ	He is no Jedi yet, but Padawan.	
	Methought—	
ANAKIN	—A Padawan, but I may speak.	
PADMÉ	Yet out of turn, remem'bring not thy place.	
	Methought nearby the lakes I could reside,	90
	By country veil'd in isolation full.	
	There shall I be most safe—	
ANAKIN	—Thy pardon, ma'am,	
	Yet I am charg'd with thy security.	
PADMÉ	This is mine home, I know it better still—	
	We have come here so I may hide within.	95
	It would be wise if thou'dst advantage take	
	Of all the knowledge I may bring to bear.	
ANAKIN	Apologies, my lady, I misspoke.	
JAMILLIA	Well then, 'tis settl'd—go upon thy way,	
	May Fate wind cords of safety 'round you both.	100

[Exeunt all but Anakin.

ANAKIN	Now have I lost my lady's heart? Nay, nay,	
	E'en though I press too hard, it is not so.	
	Vainglorious, O Anakin, art thou,	
	E'er with a childlike temper, quick to rev,	
	Resulting in my lady's cutting glance.	105
	Get hence, O boyish pride, else she shall snub	

Our ev'ry hope for love's most warm embrace.
Ne'er show the petulance she just did see,
Ne'er flash the anger that doth boil within,
Arrest the beast and bring the man to bear,   110
Give her the love you bore your mother, Shmi.
If this may be, our hearts shall sing in sync,
Voic'd with such beauty as to make heav'n talk—
Eternal blessings in my lover's ear.
Yet rush thou not impulsively thereto!   115
O, Anakin, be ever in control:
Unveil to her a gentle, caring soul,
Until she knows that you may trusted be—
Pace thou the course of love as it doth need.

                                                        [Exit.

SCENE 3.

On the planet Coruscant, in the Jedi temple.

Enter YODA, OBI-WAN KENOBI, *and several* PADAWAN YOUNGLINGS.

YODA   Reach out, sense the Force,
                Yea: around ye always 'tis,
                Use feelings ye must.

                Pray younglings, attend!
                A visitor hither comes:
                Master Obi-Wan.
PADAWANS   Good morrow to you, Master Obi-Wan.
OBI-WAN   Receive my greeting back, ye younglings small:

O'er ev'ry challenge may you swiftly rise,
And I do wish you all a merry day.   10
Now pray, forgive my brief disturbance, Master.

YODA   'Tis no disturbance,
                    But occasion for learning.
                    What help may I be?

OBI-WAN   I seek a planet, which a trusted friend   15
                    Hath told me of. His words I think not false,
                    Yet no such system shows on th'archive's maps.

YODA   Mmm, a planet whole
                    Master Obi-Wan hath lost.
                    Such embarrassment!   20

                    [To a youngling:] Liam, I prithee,
                    Draw the shades that we may see
                    The map diagram.

                    Now, your minds clear ye,
                    And together shall we find   25
                    This wayward planet.
                                        [The lights dim as a map of the
                                        galaxy is projected before them.

OBI-WAN   It should be here, by his coordinates,
                    Yet as you plainly see, naught there is found.
                    Still, gravity doth work its constant pull
                    Upon the stars throughout the area,   30
                    All focus'd on this empty-seeming place.

YODA   Gravity's shadow—
                    Yet no star and no planets
                    Are there to cast it.

Disappear'd they have,   35
Or so, at least, it seemeth.
How may't be, younglings?

PADAWAN 1 Good Master Yoda, is it possible
That someone clear'd the archive's memory?

YODA   Ha, ha! Forsooth, 'tis!   40
The minds of children amaze—
The Padawan has't.

Once th'impossible
Hath been eliminated,
What remains is truth.   45

Fly hence, Obi-Wan,
Unto gravity's center:
Your planet awaits.

Although unlikely,
The data you seek eras'd   50
Must be, warrant I.

OBI-WAN   Yet who might have the power to remove
This information from the archives, sir?
Methought such mischief was impossible.

YODA   This puzzle is most   55
Dangerous and disturbing.
Verily, 'tis true:

Only Jedi could
Remove such information,
Delete any files.   60

Yet who and wherefore,
This harder to answer is.
I'll meditate on't.

OBI-WAN   My thanks, good Master. I shall fly to see
What lies within, pull'd there by gravity.   65

[*Exeunt.*

SCENE 4.

On the planet Naboo, at the lake retreat.

Enter ANAKIN SKYWALKER *and* PADMÉ.

ANAKIN   This place is passing beautiful, beyond
What I had e'er imagin'd possible.

PADMÉ   I hither came when I was yet a child,
And would unto that island thither swim,
My fellow students and my friends withal.   5
'Twas there, within the water's cool embrace,
I felt at home, unburthen'd by my cares.
Upon the sand we all would haply lie,
And let the sun take ev'ry drop from us.
There, with my good companions, as we lay   10
And nam'd the singing birds by our own whims,
I was at peace—vast peace beyond compare.

ANAKIN   For me the sand hath never been a balm—
On Tatooine we are encumber'd by
Too much of its most coarse and unkind touch.   15
It is an ever-present irritant,
Not like the peaceful sands of thy Naboo.
Here all is soft, like cheeks upon a babe,

And smooth as sculpted alabaster too.

[He touches her arm. They kiss.

PADMÉ   Nay, it must not be so. I prithee, go—   20
Forget this most impulsive incident.

ANAKIN   The fault is mine: thy pardon, pray, bestow.
In twain mine overeager heart is rent.

[Exit Anakin.

PADMÉ   Shall these fair shores of my sweet home Naboo
Become the setting for a tale of love?   25
This Anakin doth fully dote on me,
And mayhap hath since he was but a boy.
I know not how to meet his earnest love:
The Jedi's fond attention doth confuse
The purpose of my senatorial will.   30
His eyes, which burrow deep within my soul,
Do shake the congress of my prudent wits
And thus disturb my nature politic.
His smile, which doth bring light past all degree,
Doth govern o'er my senses when it shines.   35
His spirit—vulnerable, sweet, and kind—
Doth stand before me like a man condemn'd
As though 'twere I who could his pardon grant.
In these perplexing moments doth mine heart
Quite nearly my shrewd reason overthrow,   40
Until I would unto a court of law
Present myself, and there with strength declare
That all my being hath election made
And nam'd him master of mine humble state.
But soft, this cannot be. I may not so   45
Forget myself as to be movèd by
The sweet campaigning of a lover's kiss.

There is a season for the heart's desires,
Which is but out of season presently.
This moment of the Senate's urgent need   50
Doth hold no place for sighs of fickle love.
I am resolv'd to play the senator,
Fastidious unto th'Republic's cause.
Though Anakin writes me a lover's role,
Henceforth I must perform a wiser part   55
And let the head take office o'er the heart.

                                   [Exit.

SCENE 5.

Tipoca City on the planet Kamino.

Enter RUMOR.

RUMOR   Unwittingly the lovers miss the mark,
             Naïve whilst Rumor whispers in their ears.
             Veil'd by confusion that doth lead to dark,
             E'en such a one as Anakin hath fears.
             Indeed, his heart is temper'd by cruel fire: 5
             Love may come forth, but shall by him be spoil'd.
             Eventu'lly, as Rumor doth conspire,
             Deep in mistrust their love shall be embroil'd.
             In this doth Rumor ply her merry wiles:
             Suspicion in their minds e'er I foment.   10
             Kenobi, meanwhile, searcheth on for miles,
             Aye, to my puckish will shall he be bent.
             Misunderstanding what it is he seeks,
             In truth he shall find more than he expects.

Now hurriedly he to Kamino sneaks,   15
Oblivious to Rumor's web complex.

                                           [Exit Rumor.

Enter OBI-WAN KENOBI *with the droid* R4-P17.

OBI-WAN   Unto the hidden system I have come;
              As Master Yoda guess'd, it doth exist.
              A ship, a droid, and the coordinates
              Reveal a planet that hath tried to hide.   20
              The secret system is not empty, nay,
              And gravity hath told a story true:
              Mysterious Kamino doth appear.
              Pray let us go, R4, and learn its tale.
              My scan reveals a settlement below,   25
              We shall make landing there, whate'er befall.
              This driving rain brings tiding of some ill—
              What doth this fury of the skies portend?
                      [The ship lands on the planet's surface.
R4-P17   Bleep, zing?
OBI-WAN   —I pray, remain here with the ship.
              [Exit R4-P17 as Obi-Wan enters the cloning facility.

Enter TAUN WE.

TAUN WE   Good Master Jedi, salutations, sir.   30
              Our high prime minister sends his regards.
OBI-WAN   I am expected? [*Aside:*] 'Tis impossible!
TAUN WE   Indeed, 'tis well to meet you in our home,
              Since we so long have been in touch with you.
OBI-WAN   Such wondrous mysteries I find herein!   35

TAUN WE	Give us but time, and you shall have yet more.
	Come now, and I shall show you on your way.

They approach another chamber. Enter LAMA SU.

	Our high prime minister, e'en Lama Su.
OBI-WAN	My greetings—for this welcome I give thanks.
TAUN WE	[*to Lama Su:*] I hope from now you shall more
	better know . . . 4
OBI-WAN	My name is Obi-Wan Kenobi, sir.
LAMA SU	I trust your visit here is worth its length.
	So we may then proceed with business:
	All is on schedule, as it hath been plann'd.
	Two hundred thousand we may give you now; 4
	A million further we may proffer soon.
OBI-WAN	'Tis well. You make a suitable report.

LAMA SU   Our thanks deliver we in multitudes.
             Let Master Sifo-Dyas be at peace:
             All things run to completion in their time.   50
OBI-WAN   [*aside:*] A name far past. [*To Lama Su:*] Say,
                                        Sifo-Dyas, sir?
LAMA SU   A leader of the Jedi Council, aye?
OBI-WAN   With spirit grave I must make this report:
             The Jedi Master Sifo-Dyas hath
             Been dead for lo this decade gone and past.   55
LAMA SU   More sorry I, for he would be most proud—
             The army we have built for him's immense.
OBI-WAN   An army? Did he say whom it was for?
LAMA SU   To strengthen the Republic noble's cause.
OBI-WAN   Pray, may I see this army for myself?   60
             'Tis wherefore I have to Kamino come.
TAUN WE   'Tis our delight, pray, let us thither go.
                          [*Obi-Wan, Lama Su, and Taun We
                          begin touring the clone facility.*
LAMA SU   This vast clone army we have built may be
             The best that we have e'er created yet.
             The clones themselves can think creatively,   65
             Thus are they unto droids superior,
             Their combat training is our greatest strength.
             The group you see below is five years old,
             Though you shall see they older do appear—
             'Tis growth acceleration makes it so.   70
             To speed their growth is indispensable;
             Thus clones may be mature in far less time
             Than if we were to wait a lifetime full:
             'Tis done in half the time with this technique.
             The clones are utterly obedient: 75

They take the orders giv'n sans questioning.
Their genes have through our toil been modified
To take away the independence from
The host, the subject, the original:
The bounty hunter known as Jango Fett.   80
To keep him safe, he liveth here, with us.
The only thing he did of us demand—
That is, apart from his most ample pay—
'Twas to receive a clone that he could keep:
True and unalter'd, not made pliable,   8
The replicate exact of his own genes,
Touch'd not by an accelerated growth:
This clone he raiseth as a cherish'd son.

OBI-WAN   I should delight to meet this Jango Fett.
            May such a meeting be arrang'd?   9

TAUN WE   'Tis our delight, pray, let us thither go.
                        [She leads him to Jango Fett's chamber.

                Enter JANGO FETT and BOBA FETT.

OBI-WAN   Are you the bounty hunter Jango Fett?
            I am a Jedi, Obi-Wan Kenobi.

Your clones are most remarkable, sirrah.
Methinks you must be very proud, indeed.   95

JANGO   Pride is a misstep on which one may easily slip. For
my part, I am but a humble man who seeks to wend
his way through the galaxy—I've no pride thereof.

OBI-WAN   Hath your e'er-wending way led you as far
Into th'interior as Coruscant?   100

JANGO   E'en once, mayhap twice.

OBI-WAN   'Twas once and twice and mayhap recently?

JANGO   Recently is possible—would that I could remember.

OBI-WAN   For certain, then, you must familiar be
With Jedi Master Sifo-Dyas, aye?   105

JANGO   [to Boba:] Ka Boba, rood eht so-heeck. [To Obi-Wan:]
O, Master who?
[Boba shuts a door, hiding Jango's
bounty hunter uniform.

OBI-WAN   The name is Sifo-Dyas. Was't not he
Who for this cloning task employ'd you here?

JANGO   Ne'er have I heard tell of the man.

OBI-WAN   But are you sure he is not known to you?   110

JANGO   Dear sir, mine employment came from one who was
Tyranus call'd. E'en on a moon of Bogden did he
make arrangement for to hire me.

OBI-WAN   Your words do run from strange to stranger, yea.

JANGO   Your questions at an end, now I shall ask: 115
Do you approve of this strong army?

OBI-WAN   I shall delight to see what they can do.

JANGO   They shall perform aright, e'en to the last.
Of that you may be sure, too.

OBI-WAN   I thank you, Jango, for this dialogue.   120

JANGO   Indeed, the thanks is mine—'tis e'er my pleasure

     to make acquaintance with a Jedi. [*Aside:*] Now
     we must flee, for time doth quickly run.

              [Exeunt Jango and Boba.

OBI-WAN   I have uncover'd ev'rything at last.
     [*To Taun and Lama:*] I bid ye now give me my leave

               to go 12.

     And make report unto the Jedi Council.
     Our Jedi Master, Yoda, will delight
     To hear the progress you have made herein.

LAMA SU   To strengthen the Republic noble's cause,
     The army we have built for him's immense. 13

OBI-WAN   I shall reveal to him what I have seen—
     He shall regret he did not see't himself.

LAMA SU   More sorry I, for he would be most proud—
     A leader of the Jedi Council, aye.

OBI-WAN   Regret I Master Sifo-Dyas could 13.
     Not be here to bear witness to your fruits.

LAMA SU   All things run to completion in their time:
     Let Master Sifo-Dyas be at peace.

OBI-WAN   His memory you honor, Minister.

LAMA SU   Our thanks deliver we in multitudes: 14
     A million further we may proffer soon,
     Two hundred thousand we may give you now.

OBI-WAN   And we return those thanks to thee, kind sir.
     We shall make contact soon, with further orders.

LAMA SU   All is on schedule, as it hath been plann'd. 14.
     So we may then proceed with business?

OBI-WAN   Forsooth, your operation's well in hand.

LAMA SU   I trust your visit here is worth its length.

OBI-WAN   Indeed, it hath been most enlightening.

               [Exit Lama Su.

TAUN WE   I hope from now you shall more better know   150
               Our high prime minister, e'en Lama Su.
               Come now, and I shall show you on your way.
OBI-WAN   Much gratitude for all you've shown me here—
               The soldiers you have made impress me quite.
TAUN WE   Give us but time, and you shall have yet more.   155
OBI-WAN   I understand. You have mine utmost thanks.
TAUN WE   Since we so long have been in touch with you,
               Indeed, 'tis well to meet you in our home.
OBI-WAN   Your hospitality hath been most kind.
TAUN WE   Our high prime minister sends his regards.   160
               Good Master Jedi, salutations, sir.
                                             [Exit Taun We.
OBI-WAN   Thus what was hidden now hath been reveal'd,
               Though its significance is yet conceal'd.
                                                       [Exit.

ACT III

SCENE 1.

On the planet Naboo, at the lake retreat.

Enter PADMÉ *and* ANAKIN SKYWALKER.

ANAKIN	Come, come, thou wasp: thine hidden secret shout.
PADMÉ	If I be waspish, best beware my sting.
ANAKIN	My remedy is, then, to pluck it out.
PADMÉ	If thou shalt pluck, I shall not tell the thing.
	In sooth, I do not know.
ANAKIN	—Methinks thou dost.
PADMÉ	Wilt thou perhaps a Jedi's trick employ,
	And plunder all my thoughts with ruse unjust?
ANAKIN	Nay, with such base tricks I'd not thee annoy.

Besides, such mind games would not work on thee,   1

For they are only us'd upon the weak.

PADMÉ	If thou shalt not be touch'd by jealousy,
	I'll give to thee the answer thou dost seek.
	Of my first kiss may this small tale be sung:

Mine age was twelve, and he was Palo nam'd.   1

A legislative program for the young

Did mark the place where first my lips were tam'd.

A handsome boy, and older by some years,

With raven's eyes and curly hair of brown.

ANAKIN	Thou hast spoke long enough to burn mine ears. 2
	So what of him? How did he let you down?
	What was his error or his fatal blunder?
	Or was it he whose interest did fade?
	Aye, wert thou maid or unmade? O, you wonder!
PADMÉ	No wonder, nay; but certainly a maid. 2

	To public service my direction led,	
	Whilst he became an artist in Naboo.	
ANAKIN	Mayhap 'twas he who acted with his head.	
PADMÉ	Thou dost not care for politicians, true?	
ANAKIN	Nay, there are two or three I do prefer—	30
	They are an ample feast to suit my taste.	
	There is one dish of which I'm yet unsure,	
	Whose flavor is with zest and spices lac'd.	
	Yet, by my troth, I think the system broken:	
	'Tis not the cogs, but 'tis the whole machine.	35
PADMÉ	How should it run, if in thy words 'twere spoken?	
ANAKIN	They all should sit together and convene—	
	Discussing ev'ry matter of the state—	
	And make agreement as to what is best	
	For ev'ry creature, whether small or great:	40
	Then on their findings should their actions rest.	
PADMÉ	Yea, as thou just hast said we surely do,	

	Yet trouble comes when all cannot agree.	
ANAKIN	Then those who disagree are most untrue,	
	And must be made to sing in common key.	4
PADMÉ	By whom? Which choirmaster wouldst thou name?	
ANAKIN	Someone who would conduct the group aright.	
PADMÉ	Wouldst thou hold that baton?	
ANAKIN	—'Twas not my claim.	
PADMÉ	Then someone else?	
ANAKIN	—Aye, someone wise, with might.	
PADMÉ	Thy tune doth sound most like dictatorship.	5
ANAKIN	If it would work, I'd sing its melody.	
PADMÉ	Thou mockest me, I see it in thy lip.	
ANAKIN	Nay, I intend no sharp disharmony.	
	'Twould be unwise a senator to mock,	
	For mockingbirds do whistle scornful airs.	5
PADMÉ	Your sly refrain upon mine heart doth knock,	
	And helpeth to unburthen me from cares.	

Enter a herd of SHAAKS.

ANAKIN	[*aside:*] My love, my joy, my senator, my queen!	
	To hear her laugh doth set my soul to sigh.	
	What light is light, if Padmé be not seen?	6
	What joy is joy, if Padmé be not by?	
	[*To Padmé:*] Let us have sport, and merry make the day.	
PADMÉ	These beasts are beautiful, yet can be rough.	
	May Jedi over such as these hold sway?	
ANAKIN	Methinks my skill and strength shall be enough.	6
	[*Anakin jumps onto a shaak and begins riding it.*	
PADMÉ	Behold how like its master thou dost ride!	

Forsooth, thou hast a senator impress'd.

ANAKIN The creature is with vigor well supplied,
And by some rage it now doth seem possess'd.

[*The shaak throws Anakin to the ground.*

PADMÉ My strong protector, O, mine Anakin!   70
My soul did cry as I beheld his fall.

[*Padmé runs to Anakin. Exeunt shaaks.*

Speak thou, good Ani, hast thou injur'd been?
Be thou not broken by this creature's gall.

ANAKIN Ha, ha, my chuck, I do but jest by schemes.
And yet thine eyes—they show thy care unfurl'd,   75
They are the books, the arts, the academes,
That show, contain, and nourish all the world.

PADMÉ By heav'n, I am reliev'd that thou art well:
The fear that shook me so is turn'd to joy.

ANAKIN Be not afeard, or if thou art, then tell—   80
Together we shall all thy fears destroy.

PADMÉ Thou art my safeguard strong, my Jedi Knight.
Now since thou art yet whole, say: shall we dine?

ANAKIN To follow all thy steps brings me delight—
If 'tis your will to eat, then it is mine.   85

[*They proceed to a table to sup.*

PADMÉ What canst thou say that shall my mirth arouse?

ANAKIN Mayhap this need-born phrase we Jedi say—
A technique we from time to time espouse—
"Determinèd negotiations," yea.

PADMÉ Determinèd negotiations, what?   90
What doth it mean, for I've not heard of it?

ANAKIN It doth imply negotiations, but:
Those manag'd by a lightsaber, to wit.

[*Aside:*] I know I love in vain, no hope thereof;

Yet in this captious and intenible sieve   9

I still pour in the waters of my love—

It is the very hope for which I live.

Now bring the Force upon this happy scene,

I shall employ its pow'r my lass to tease.

                   [Anakin uses the Force to lift a

                         pear and bring it to him.

PADMÉ   Such tricks do render all my thoughts serene.   10

ANAKIN   'Tis well, they'd not put Obi-Wan at ease.

                   [He cuts a slice of pear and, using

                       the Force, passes it to her.

PADMÉ   This fruit thou sendest me the Force withal

Shall fall most pleasantly upon my lips.

The thanks I render thee are far too small

To quite express what from my spirit slips.   10

Pretty and witty, wild, and yet, too, gentle:

Thou fashion'd art of paradox, in part.

Yet such faint praise can be but detrimental

Unto the noble man thou truly art.

Thou art a treasur'd and a worthy friend,   11

Protector of my life, though all unplann'd.

If things were chang'd, perhaps love would transcend

And tame my wild heart to thy loving hand.

ANAKIN   The closer we become, the more I ache,

To be sans you would steal my very breath.   11

The kiss thou gave, which I did gladly take,

Doth move upon my passions as a death.

Can I go forward when my heart is here,

The heart that thou, with lips, have turn'd to scar?

Thou art a specter, ghost to my good cheer,   12

Tormenting me by haunting pow'r bizarre.

What may I do? What shall I say to thee?
What speech will exorcise your maiden doubt
And turn the spirit of your love to me?
But speak the word: thy servant is devout.   125

PADMÉ   Love like a shadow flies, pursu'd too soon.

ANAKIN   Is't possible that thou dost long for me?
If thou dost suffer love, then 'tis a boon:
But say 'tis so and we may joinèd be.

PADMÉ   We two may not within one love be knit.   130
For love is blind and lovers cannot see
The pretty follies that themselves commit.
How pretty would such follies in us be?
It is not possible.

ANAKIN   —O, say not so!
The course of true love never did run smooth.   135
What blossom without weeds did ever grow?
I prithee listen, let my reason soothe.
This bud of love, by Naboo's ripening breath,
May prove a beauteous flower of which we'll boast.

PADMÉ   Nay, thou shalt listen, my soul warranteth: 140
The tempter or the tempted, who sins most?
The vision thou dost proffer suits us not,
Thine honor nor my station, neither one.
Reality it seems thou hast forgot,
For us to love would mean us both undone.   145
Thou art a Jedi, I a senator,
If thou wouldst follow thy thoughts to their end
Then wouldst thou with my judgment straight concur:
I am not made for lover, but for friend.
This must be so, regardless how we feel,   150
And how our passions move toward each other.

ANAKIN   There thou hast given thy confession real:
            Thou lovest me—we yearn for one another!

PADMÉ   Thy future I would never take from thee,
            And thus oppose the thread of Fate's design.   15
            I pray thee, do not fall in love with me,
            For I am falser than vows made in wine.

ANAKIN   And yet thou ask'st that which I may not do:
            To speak mine heart as though it were my mind.
            Would that I mine affection could eschew,   16
            And change as quickly as the moon unkind.
            Yet 'tis not so.

PADMÉ   —I shall not bow to this:
            The pressure and the childish, nagging voice.
            Thy love, and not thy spite, should meet my kiss.

ANAKIN   Belike there is, as yet, another choice.   16
            Mayhap in some enclosèd, private place,
            We could agree to meet and be as one.
            There could I see the beauty of thy face,
            Our secret safe, we would not be undone.

PADMÉ   Yet would this render all our days a lie,   17
            A lie our souls would never let us keep.
            Thou couldst not live in such a way, nor I—
            Our love by such a bargain is made cheap.
            Thou couldst not want that, couldst thou, Anakin?
            I know that thou art made of better stuff.   17

ANAKIN   Indeed, it would destroy us both therein.
            Thou hast o'errul'd my passion well enough.
            Alas, there's some ill galaxy that reigns,
            I must be patient till the heavens look
            With an aspect more favorable. Chains   18
            Would be more comfort than this hope forsook.

                                        [Exit Anakin.

PADMÉ O, time! Thou must untangle this, not I;
      It is too hard a knot for me t'untie.

                 [Exit Padmé.

SCENE 2.

Tipoca City, on the planet Kamino.

Enter OBI-WAN KENOBI.

OBI-WAN For answers to Kamino did I come,
      And such I did receive in quantities:
      Two hundred thousand answers met me here.
      Yet with this army comes more questions on—
      What was it Sifo-Dyas hop'd to do?   5
      And who is this Tyranus Fett speaks of?
      I must make contact with the Council next!

Enter R4-P17.

R4-P17   Blip, whoop.
OBI-WAN   —R4, I bid thee set code five
      For Coruscant, care of the elders' home.

Enter YODA *and* MACE WINDU *on balcony.*

      Good Masters, I've establish'd contact with 10
      Kamino, and with its prime minister.
      They use a bounty hunter, Jango Fett,
      And by him build an army made from clones.
      Mine instincts do inform me Jango Fett

             Is e'en the selfsame bounty hunter who   15
             Would be assassin of the senator.

MACE   Do you believe the cloners are involv'd
             In this nerfar'ous plot? I'll fly away
             Myself to work them woe if it be so.

OBI-WAN   Nay, Master, for they could not gain thereby.   20

YODA   Avoid assumption,
             Obi-Wan, we need your mind
             Most open to be.

             When clear are your thoughts,
             Discovery of villains   25
             In this plot follows.

OBI-WAN   Indeed, good Master. They did make report
             That Master Sifo-Dyas was the one
             Who did request an army of the clones.
             This deed he did perform ten years ago,   30
             Upon request of the Galactic Senate.
             Yet 'twas my memory that he was kill'd
             Ere then—say, did the Council authorize
             Creation of an army led by clones?

MACE   Nay, nay. Whoe'er it was the order plac'd   35
             Hath drunk a juice the Council did not serve.

YODA   If you can bring him,
             This bounty hunter vicious,
             Question him we will.

OBI-WAN   Indeed, I shall report when he is mine.   40

                                [Exeunt Obi-Wan and R4-P17.

YODA   Most blind we have been,
             If this army's creation
             We ne'er did foresee.

MACE   Belike 'tis time to tell the Senate that

The Council's aptitude to use the Force   45
Hath been diminish'd; aye, in the extreme.
A shock to th'system this indeed shall be,
Yet pride is worse than deep humility.

YODA   Only one, e'en he—
          The vile dark lord of the Sith—   50
          Knoweth our weakness.

          If, then, the Senate
          Of this fault are giv'n to know,
          Our enemies grow.

                                        [*Exeunt.*

SCENE 3.
On the planet Naboo.

Enter ANAKIN SKYWALKER.

ANAKIN   What nightmares viciously infect my mind?
          My mother, gracious woman, kind and sweet—
          She cries for me as though rack'd by some plague,
          By some disease or deadly pestilence
          She hath been set upon—O, mother dear!   5
          Thine agony resounds throughout my soul
          And doth contaminate my better self.
          So sleep is vanish'd all too suddenly
          And I do rise too early in the night,
          As doth the bile that rises in my soul.   10

Enter PADMÉ.

PADMÉ   Thou hast not slept aright these many nights,
               If thou wouldst rest anon, I'll give thee peace.

ANAKIN   Thy presence doth turn wrongs into their rights,
               'Tis peace itself and brings my mind release.

PADMÉ   Thou had a visitation of a spirit—   1
               A demon of the night to work you woe.
               If thou wouldst fain recount, I'd haply hear it,
               And share the pain that thou dost undergo.

ANAKIN   A Jedi should be strong, with nightmares none.

PADMÉ   I heard thee in the night, most piteous.   2

ANAKIN   It was my mother: weak, distress'd, undone,
               The vision rank was passing venomous.
               Yet there is more: 'tis not just boyish fright—
               My mother suffering, which I did see,
               The sounds and scenes that came to me by night   2
               Are echoes of some present misery.
               She was as plain to me as thou art now,
               And is the subject of some grievous pain.
               To give thee my protection is my vow,
               Yet such made I in boyhood's zeal most vain.   3
               I must forsake that vow and go from thee:
               I was still boy when first our tale began,
               But now, by mine own mother's agony,
               The boy is gone, and so departs the man.

PADMÉ   If thou shalt go, then I shall go withal,   3
               Thy path shall be my path, thy pain as well.

ANAKIN   If I could choose, I would not need this call:
               A mother's anguish doth my soul compel.

PADMÉ   Naboo we leave, with all its dreamlike sheen,
               And greet the morn to fly to Tatooine!   4

                                        [Exeunt.

SCENE 4.

On the planet Kamino, in Tipoca City.

Enter JANGO FETT *and* BOBA FETT, *preparing their ship to depart.*

JANGO   Now all's prepar'd, and we shall fly anon. The prying
            of the Jedi soon is past. 'Tis true Kamino hath provided
            most lucrative and simple employment. Yet now the
            welcome hath been made unwell, and thus I fly.

BOBA   Behold, father, the Jedi cometh!   5

Enter OBI-WAN KENOBI, *brandishing his lightsaber.*

JANGO   Pray, Boba, flee aboard the ship! Now die, thou
            Jedi half-man.
                              [As he flies into the air with his jetpack,
                                    Jango shoots at Obi-Wan.

OBI-WAN   The bounty hunter flies—his lasers, too—
            Yet I am quick and parry easily.
            His boy hath now the ship engag'd to leave,   10
            But Obi-Wan hath writ another end.

JANGO   Lasers hath not giv'n you trouble enow, yet may my
            rocket's thunder still enthrall.
                              [Jango fires a rocket at Obi-Wan,
                                whose lightsaber is knocked from his hand.

OBI-WAN   Alas, what blast—my lightsaber is gone!

BOBA   Now I shall join the fray—feel the fire of *Slave One*'s   15
            deadly aim.
                              [Boba fires upon Obi-Wan from within the ship.

OBI-WAN   The villain flies to me—feel thou my kick!

If we in combat shall meet hand to hand,
I'll warrant thou shalt by me bested be.

JANGO   In combat you are skill'd, Jedi. E'en now, feel   20
               all the power of my wire!

                               [Jango shoots a cable around
                                   Obi-Wan's wrists and flies away.

OBI-WAN   'Tis but a merry ride—is this thy worst?
               Though by this wire thou pullest me along,
               This platform's pillars shall be stronger still.

                         [Obi-Wan stops his fall by tying the cable
                           around a pillar, stopping Jango's flight.

JANGO   My jetpack gone, I take a raucous slam. Lo, now   25
               the Jedi comes again—he kicketh me, I fall!

OBI-WAN   He falls, yet is still bound to me by wire—
               Thus his fall doth become mine own anon.
               O, Obi-Wan, say wilt thou never learn?

                         [Together they begin to fall down
                           the side of the landing platform.

JANGO   This shall not be the end of Jango Fett. Let these,   30
               mine armor'd blades, quickly stop my fall. From there,
               may I untwine this Jedi from myself. Yea, thus the Fetts
               do win the day.

OBI-WAN   He hath releas'd me. Thus my fall is free,
               But still have I this wire wherewith to work.   35
               I prithee, Fate, knit me a mighty cord:
               Let your cord and this wire be e'en as one!
               The wire I toss—it catches 'round a pipe!
               Again, Fate weaves for me a close escape.

                         [Jango spies over the precipice and sees
                           no sign of Obi-Wan.

JANGO   Yea, now the Jedi is dispatch'd unto the briny depths—   40

farewell, most weak adversary. To the ship, and we
shall swiftly depart.

OBI-WAN   This portal may I take back to the platform,
And fight another round with Jango Fett.

                                        [Obi-Wan enters the lift.

BOBA   My father hath defeated the Jedi scum. Thus, we go!   45

                                *[Exeunt Jango and Boba as their
                                        ship starts to fly. Obi-Wan reenters.*

OBI-WAN   I am too late to stop this Jango Fett
And render him unto the Council wise.
Yet by this keen device he may be mine—

                                *[Obi-Wan throws a tracking device
                                        onto Jango Fett's ship.*

Thus do your work and track his fleeing ship:
I slip this in though he gives me the slip.   50

                                                        [Exit.

SCENE 5.

On the planet Tatooine.

Enter PADMÉ, ANAKIN SKYWALKER, *and* R2-D2.
Enter WATTO *severally.*

ANAKIN   O, chut, chut, Watto. Ding me chasa holp'.
WATTO   Gibudah, eh? Du bana biotah?
Nuh chada Jedi? Robata, nuhdoo!
ANAKIN   *[aside:]* He thinketh I have come to bring him grief,
For though he is not swift of wit, he knows
The dress and tools that make a Jedi Knight.
Now, to't. *[To Watto:]* Me bosha di Shmi Skywalker.
WATTO   'Tis Ani? Little Ani? Aye, 'tis you!

             Most verily you like a bud did sprout.

             A Jedi now, indeed? Mayhap you could   10

             Give me persistence with some brigands vile

             Who owe me money? Show your Jedi strength?

ANAKIN   My mother is mine only purpose here.

WATTO   Indeed, your Shmi. She is no longer mine.

             I sold her.

ANAKIN   —Sold her?

WATTO   —Years ago 'twas done.   15

             Apologies, dear Ani, but so goes

             The straying: business is business.

             I sold her to a moisture farmer, Lars,

             And thereupon I heard he married her.

             Sand's not so harsh but love may make it smooth.   20

ANAKIN   Canst tell me where my mother may be found?

WATTO   'Tis far, beyond Mos Eisley, I believe.

ANAKIN   I fain would know where.

WATTO   —Obsoletely, aye!

             Pray, come and I'll my chronicles review.

                     [Anakin and Watto walk aside.

PADMÉ   For this dear friend, this precious Anakin,   25

             Mine heart doth worry with a troubl'd beat.

             He doth attempt to show an aspect strong,

             But in his visage doth his fear emerge

             As though 'twere tattoo'd on his gallant face.

             And though he loves me, when he loves me not,   30

             Chaos is come again. Such do I fear,

             For he is like a sail upon the wind,

             E'er buffeted upon the roiling waves

             Of his most tender and e'er-changing moods.

             Row steady, captain of my stormy heart,   35

Let not thy rudder turn at ev'ry surge.

R2-D2   [*aside:*] O, would that some solace could provide
Unto this lady, tender, sweet, and true.

           [*Exit Watto as Anakin returns.*

ANAKIN   My mother is not here, but farther on.
Wilt thou go with me, gentle lady? Speak.   4

PADMÉ   I will, and shall—pray, let us go anon
And find the one thou earnestly dost seek.
I prithee, good R2, stay with the ship,
This is a journey we shall make alone.
Remain, and here our vessel strong equip,   4
That when 'tis done, we may from here be flown.

R2-D2   Beep, squeak, beep, whistle, meep, beep, whistle, woo.
[*Aside:*] Loath am I to make my departure hence,
For e'en a fool as R2 can infer
The trouble that awaits on Tatooine.   5
I do not know how this grim tale shall end,
Though hope doth still resound within my wires.
Aye, peradventure all may still end well.

           [*Exit R2-D2 as Padmé and Anakin
           journey toward the Lars homestead.*

ANAKIN   Lo, thither in the distance I do see
The homestead whereof Watto spoke of late.   5
Belike my mother waits there presently,
Although mine instincts other truths relate.

               Enter C-3PO.

C-3PO   Holla! May I some honest service render?
My name is call'd C—

ANAKIN   —Threepio, 'tis thee?

| C-3PO | The maker, even Master Anakin! | 60 |

                I knew you would return to me one day.

                And Lady Padmé, by my droidly troth!

PADMÉ   Fair greetings, Threepio.

C-3PO   —O, bless my circuits!

                Forsooth, it doth me well to see you here.

ANAKIN   I have return'd to see my mother, Shmi.   65

C-3PO   Indeed. [*Aside:*] O etiquette, O protocol!

                [*To Anakin:*] Perhaps it would be best to walk indoors.

                There may my master Lars her tale unfold.

Enter OWEN LARS *and* BERU WHITESUN *as the group
enters the Lars homestead.*

OWEN   C-3PO?

C-3PO   —Good Master Owen, might

                I introduce two noble visitors?   70

ANAKIN   Know ye my name? I'm Anakin Skywalker.

OWEN   I Owen Lars, and this my lass, Beru.

BERU   Good morrow, sir.

PADMÉ   —And I am Padmé call'd.

OWEN   [*to Anakin:*] I' faith, your name is known to me,

                                    good sir.

                It seemeth I am stepbrother to you.   75

                Methought that you might someday here arrive:

                That day hath come.

ANAKIN   —Yet is my mother here?

Enter CLIEGG LARS.

CLIEGG   Alack, for this must be the answer: nay.

My name is Cliegg, and Shmi is my dear wife.
Pray, step within, for I have much to say.   8(

ANAKIN [*aside:*] Confusion! I, who ne'er had family,
In searching for the one hath found three more?
I did not seek a wealth of relatives,
Such riches ne'er did dwell in my desires.
Still they are here, and fortune should be mine,   8
Except my mother doth her richness hide.

                    [*They enter the Lars homestead
                        and sit at a table.*

CLIEGG I prithee, rest awhile and hear my tale:
'Twas just e'er dawn not many days ago,
They came from nowhere, like a sudden storm:
The Tusken Raiders in their vicious might.   9(
Your mother had departed early on,
As was her wont, to gather mushrooms, which
Upon the moisture vaporators grow.
The story that her footprints do impart
Relate that she had reach'd the half-point home   9.
When she by Tusken Raiders was beset.
The Tuskens do as humans walk and talk,
Yet in their hearts are fill'd with viciousness
That doth befit a monster, not a man.
Full thirty able souls did venture forth   10(
To find her; only four of us return'd.
Such slaughter mine eyes never wish'd to see,
Brought on by their brutality extreme.
Yea, I would thither be a'searching still
Were not my leg a victim of their wrath.   10
I cannot ride again until I heal,
And then shall I resume the search once more.

My stubborn heart will not admit defeat,
Though she is gone for lo this full moon past.
I would not give up hope, though little hope   110
Remains that she has strength t'endure this long.

[Anakin rises.

OWEN   Pray, whither would you go, O, Anakin?

ANAKIN   To find a mother by some other means
Than telling tales of lost and shatter'd hope.

CLIEGG   Your mother must be dead, son, let it be.   115

ANAKIN   Acceptance is a fashion ill-befitting—
Yea, such a garment I'll not rush to wear.
I say, if you would talk of letting be,
Then let me be and do restrain me not.
You are prepar'd to say that she is lost,   120
But I shall speak not so till I have proof.
My mother to the last I'll strive to find,
Thus not to dance too quickly on her grave.

[Exeunt Cliegg Lars, Owen Lars,
Beru Whitesun, and C-3PO.

PADMÉ   O, troubl'd soul, how may I give thee aid,
And what words speak that I may succor give?   125

ANAKIN   I prithee, stay thou here, be not dismay'd,
These people have kind souls, as I do live.
Thou shalt be safe shouldst thou with them remain.

PADMÉ   Courageous man! Mine heart with thine's entwin'd.

ANAKIN   This moment doth beget a bitter pain: 130
My love I leave, another love to find.

[Exeunt.

SCENE 6.

Outer space, near the planet Geonosis.

Enter RUMOR.

RUMOR   Bold Anakin doth search both near and far,
               E'en as his mother groans on Tatooine.
               His sharp confusion, fear, and anger are
               Old friends full welcome unto Rumor's scene.
               Let him in his despair, at his young age,   5
               Deny the Jedi training that he knows,
               Thus spend his fury, satisfy his rage,
               His mother to defend by hearty blows.
               E'en thus doth Rumor lead him to the edge,
               Burn deep within the furnace of his mind.   10
               And thus, for love of mother, shall he pledge
               To maim and kill whomever he may find.
               The scene here doth return to Obi-Wan,
               Led by a small device to distant shore,
               Ere he hath left, his mind shall wildly run—   15
               So Rumor multiplies her whispers more.
               Come ye unto the scene: behold the Fetts
               Endeavor to destroy the Jedi Knight,
               Now Obi-Wan is caught within their nets.
               Enough of talk: bear witness to the fight!   20
                                              [*Exit Rumor.*

Enter JANGO FETT *and* BOBA FETT *on balcony, in ship. Enter* OBI-WAN
    KENOBI *and* R4-P17 *below, pursuing in Obi-Wan's ship.*

BOBA   My father, behold! It seemeth we are track'd.

JANGO	Lo, the knave's alive, and with trickery hath placèd a homing beacon upon our hull. My son, be thou at ease and take care: unto the field of asteroids we'll fly and there unfold surprises enow for him. 25
R4-P17	Whoop, zip!
OBI-WAN	—The knave employeth seismic charges. I shall make swift maneuvers to survive.

[Jango's seismic charges begin to explode as Obi-Wan flies through.

What pow'rs hath humans wrought that can bring such
Destruction to such asteroids as these?
These weapons we've created have such might   30
As would impress the gods in all their heights.
Now, as these potent weapons turn on me,
I sense their magnitude with new respect.
The asteroids do burst to bits an 'twere
A mass of sand assail'd by ocean's flood—   35
What strange occurrence hath befallen us
When we create that which creation wrecks,
When we hath brought to life that which aids death.

JANGO	E'en so the man doth follow on apace. Disdain doth rise within my gorge, for this Jedi is not easily dissuaded. 40 Yet I shall still prevail, as I within this asteroid fly.
OBI-WAN	Through tunnels vast, through fields of asteroids: Still there I shall pursue thee, Jango Fett.
JANGO	Now we emerge as he still flies within. This asteroid shall serve as hiding spot. He doth fly out but, lo, a 45 difference: he who was chas'd—e'en me—is now he who chaseth.
BOBA	What cunning, Father, aye! Pray, strike him with thy fiery blast!

[*Jango fires at Obi-Wan.*

OBI-WAN   At once I am reminded wherefore I   50
             Am not inclin'd to fly. Such madness, O!
             The ship is struck—R4, canst thou repair't?

BOBA   Thou hittest the mark!

JANGO   Indeed, the first hit hath been struck, and
             presently shall I finish the Jedi.   5.

                        [*Jango fires a heat-seeking rocket at Obi-Wan.*

OBI-WAN   Alas, from bad to worse! Heat-seeking shells
             Fly swiftly on toward mine harried ship.
             The very heat that gives my body life
             And that keen fire that powers my fleet ship
             Do now betray me, even unto death.   60
             R4, I call on thee, good droid: prepare
             To jettison the spare part cannisters.

R4-P17   Bleep, whoop!

OBI-WAN   —I prithee, send them forth e'en now!

                        [*The spare parts are released and the
                        rockets hit them, exploding upon contact.*

JANGO   A blessed sight, eh, Boba? 'Tis so: we shall not be
             troubl'd by his like again, I'll warrant.   6

                        [*Exeunt Jango and Boba.*

OBI-WAN   Well done, R4. The strong explosion hath
             Giv'n cover to our hidden purposes:
             First to survive, which we have managèd,
             And second, to pursue this Jango Fett,
             And third, to find where hurriedly he flies,   7
             And last of all, to learn who waiteth there:
             The unknown bard of this conspiracy.
             Let us fly hence, the bounty hunter track
             Unto the planet, recogniz'd by mine

Own chart as Geonosis. Quickly, go!   75
And let us see what wonders wait below.
Behold, R4, those Federation ships—
How vast the sum of them, all in one spot.
Let us make landing: surely 'tis the place.

[They land on Geonosis.

I prithee, brave R4, stay with the ship.   80
I shall conceal myself, and as I hide
The thing that we do seek may be reveal'd.

[Exit R4-P17.

Here in this hall of stone I shall be hid,
With rocky walls full high and hard to climb,
And the place death, considering who I am.   85
Behold, what industry doth run within—
A factory for making battle droids.
Whate'er the Federation hath design'd,
It seems this is the operation's base.
But soft, I hear a group that comes anon.   90

[Obi-Wan hides behind an arras.

Enter COUNT DOOKU, NUTE GUNRAY, DAULTAY DOFINE,
WAT TAMBOR, SHU MAI, SAN HILL, *and other* CONSPIRATORS.

DOOKU   The pow'rful Commerce Guild together with
               The Corporate Alliance must both be
               Persuaded to be signatories to
               Our treaty. Only thus our plans succeed.
NUTE   What of the senator from small Naboo?   95
               Hath our assassin executed her?
               I shall not sign your treaty, sir, until
               Her head doth ornament my chamber desk.

DOOKU   I shall fulfill my word, good viceroy, and
           Deliver unto you the prize you seek.   100

WAT   With these new battle droids that we have built,
           Your army shall best all that they do meet:
           The finest troop within the galaxy.

OBI-WAN   [aside:] Some treason, this! Count Dooku doth conspire
           To overthrow the strong Republic with   105
           These wretched villains, furthering his cause.

DOOKU   As I explain'd to you ere now, more than
           Ten thousand systems shall join with our cause
           Once I have your support, good gentlemen.

SHU   What you propose could be constru'd, dear sir,   11
           As treason in the uttermost degree.

WAT   The Techno Union army waits upon
           Your pleasure, Count, and doth stand by to serve.

SAN   The Banking Clan shall sign your treaty, Count.

DOOKU   'Tis well. Our allies of the Federation   11
           Have pledg'd their strong support. When all their droids
           Are match'd to yours, our army shall surpass
           All others in the galaxy. And the
           Conclusion is the Jedi are o'erwhelm'd.

In practice let us put it presently.   120
The game is won, the checkmate shall be ours:
The pawns are now in place, and we, the kings,
Perforce rush forth to take the Jedi Knights.
With such a move the weak Republic shall
Be lost, and bow to those demands we make.   125

        [Exeunt all but Obi-Wan, who emerges
                from his hiding place.

OBI-WAN   Mine ears do burn by treason's wicked flame.
A band of traitorous conspirators
Doth seek to bring th'Republic to its knees,
And in the doing rout the Jedi, too.
Was e'er such villainy as this design'd?   130
Was e'er such treachery as this conceiv'd?
Was e'er such perfidy as this begun?
Was e'er such wrongdoing as this devis'd?
Conspiracy upon conspiracy
Doth grow such that I find myself amaz'd.   135
Attempt on the senator's dear life
Turn'd to a bounty hunter's keen pursuit,
The bounty hunter led to cloners' art,
News of an army order'd for th'Republic.
From there the bounty hunter led once more   140
Unto this scene of greatest menace yet:
A plot to overthrow all we hold dear,
Including e'en the Jedi Order, too.
With haste I must report this evil scheme,
Mayhap to save us from a vile regime.   145

                        [Exit.

ACT
IV

SCENE 1.
On the planet Tatooine.

Enter ANAKIN SKYWALKER.

ANAKIN   My tale of woe may yet to madness run.
                Departing from my newfound family,
                My way upon the dunes of Tatooine
                I sped to douse the blazing in mine heart
                And rac'd to find my mother and her captors.   5
                The mocking setting suns of Tatooine
                Refus'd to share their light and give me aid,
                As if to say dark deeds deserve dark night.
                The rocks I pass'd assail'd me with their taunts,
                Assuring me they'd witness'd stronger griefs.   10
                Stone arches underneath which I did fly
                Seem'd to adjure me to make greater haste.
                At dusk I found a roving Jawa band,
                And did convince them that they must disclose
                Whatever knowledge of my mother's plight   15
                They had discover'd in the journeying.
                They steer'd me to the Raiders' settlement,
                Where, with a Jedi's stealth I've enter'd in.
                From tent to tent I search, and sense her here:
                My mother, still alive though suffering.   20

He comes upon SHMI SKYWALKER, *who is bound and injured.*

                Alack, sweet mother, I'll untie these knots.
                Kind mother, speak, and let me hear thy voice.
SHMI   'Tis Ani? Is it thee, my boy grown up?

ANAKIN	Forsooth, 'tis I, and thou art safe at last.
SHMI	O Ani, thou art handsomer a thing 25
	Than ere these mother's eyes did hope to see.
	My son, my little boy, my full-grown man.
	My feeble heart doth beat with earnest pride:
	No other wish had I but to see thee.
ANAKIN	I've miss'd thee so.
SHMI	—My life is now complete. 30
	I love thee, Anakin. Now may I rest.
	Commend me to mine husband: O, farewell!

[Shmi dies.

ANAKIN	O, agony, O, melancholy vast.
	My mother, O! She should have died hereafter,
	There would have been a time for such a word. 35
	Tomorrow and tomorrow and tomorrow
	Creeps in this petty pace from day to day
	To the last syllable of recorded time,
	And all our yesterdays have lighted fools
	The way to dusty death. On, on, lightsaber! 40
	Since I could not my mother longer know,
	Could not by mine own hands assuage her pain
	Or bring to her a moment of relief,
	There is no time for grieving neither, nay.
	My grief instead shall turn to sweet revenge, 45
	The sadness be transform'd to hate and rage.
	One life she gave to satisfy their thirst,
	Yet my thirst knows no bounds: no simple drink
	Can slake the dehydration of my soul,
	Can quench the drought that hath dried up my heart. 50
	The only swill that satisfies tonight
	Shall be the essence that gives life to each.

Yea, Tusken Raiders, ready ye the cups:
I'll swallow ye, be drunk upon your blood!

       [Exit Anakin to sounds of screams.

Enter YODA *and* MACE WINDU, *on balcony.*

MACE   What troubles you, good Master Yoda? Say,   55
               What phantom menace in your mind doth rise?
YODA   'Tis pain, suffering,
               Death all around. Something vile
               Hath happen'd, in sooth.

Young Skywalker, O!   60
Another's pain he borrows—
Terrible sorrows.

                                        [*Exeunt.*

SCENE 2.

On the planets Geonosis, Tatooine, and Coruscant.

Enter OBI-WAN KENOBI *and* R4-P17.

OBI-WAN   My transmitter doth operate aright,
                 Yet we receive no signal in return.
                 Belike yon Coruscant is too far gone.
                 R4, canst thou the power yet increase?

R4-P17   Zing, whoop.

OBI-WAN   —Some other plan we shall devise.   5
                 Mayhap we may reach Anakin, who is
                 Much closer, still residing on Naboo.
                 [*Into transmitter:*] I prithee, Anakin, canst thou hear me?
                 'Tis Obi-Wan Kenobi. Pray, respond.
                 [*To R4-P17:*] He is not on Naboo, R4. Where, then?   10
                 If, peradventure, I increase the range
                 He may yet be discover'd. I do hope
                 That naught of ill hath happen'd to the boy.
                 A-ha! There 'tis, his tracking signal, yea—
                 But what is this? It comes from Tatooine!   15
                 What childish folly doth he seek therein?
                 Mine order was on Naboo to remain.

R4-P17   Whoop, zing, bleep, whoop.

OBI-WAN   —We have but little time.
                 I prithee, Anakin, dost thou hear me?

Enter R2-D2 *on balcony, receiving message.*

My long-range transmitter hath been destroy'd.   20
Deliver this dispatch to Coruscant.
                              [Exeunt Obi-Wan and R4-P17.

R2-D2   I shall! For I alone within the ship
               Am here, my master's message to receive.
                              [Exit R2-D2.

Enter ANAKIN SKYWALKER *holding* SHMI SKYWALKER'*s body. Enter*
PADMÉ, CLIEGG LARS, OWEN LARS, *and* BERU WHITESUN *severally.*

ANAKIN   My mother, dead and wrapp'd within this shroud,
                I bring to this, her final resting place.   25
                Good souls, I pray, do we all holy rites:
                Let there be sung a funereal dirge.
                The dead with charity enclos'd in sand:
                And then unto the ship, and then Naboo,
                Where ne'er from Tatooine arriv'd more grief.   30
                              [Owen sings a funeral dirge.
OWEN   [*sings:*] She is dead and gone, lady,
                She is dead and gone.
                At her head a sandy turf,
                And her heels a stone.
                She is far beyond, lady,   35
                She is far beyond.
                Lady whom we knew in life,
                Lady more than fond.
                She is pass'd and done, lady,
                She is pass'd and done.   40
                Mourn'd by those who weep for her,
                Mourn'd by her own son.

CLIEGG   Where'er thou goest, from this mortal coil,
             The place is better, for thou there dost dwell.
             Of loving partners thou wert ever first: 45
             The best a man could find i'the galaxy.
             Farwell my love, my hope, my joy, my all—
             My gratitude complete take thou with thee.

ANAKIN   I had not strength to save thee, mother dear,
             My might was not sufficient—still, I vow   50
             That nevermore I'll fail when fac'd with death.
             Already I do miss thee, past all sense.

CLIEGG   Now we'll away, to spend ourselves in grief.

                              [Exeunt Cliegg Lars, Owen Lars,
                                       and Beru Whitesun.

ANAKIN   What anguish lies within my weary soul!
             The mother whom I lov'd—do love, would love—   55
             Hath been remov'd. How shall I e'er be whole?
             O, monstrous Fate that knits our lives above,
             And doth not condescend to look below
             And see what knots its tangled string doth weave.
             Would that I could its crushing grip forego   60
             And be its master, so to gain reprieve
             From all the mocking twists that Fate doth give.
             One day I shall rise far beyond this fate,
             Rise thither where all do forever live.
             Until that day, I curse this dark estate.   65

PADMÉ   I bid thee, wilt thou come inside and eat?

ANAKIN   I shall inside to fix the speeder, aye,
             For as I rode the shifter did o'erheat.
             Life doth seem simpler when a project's nigh.
             There's little broken but my skill may fix.   70
             Yet I could not fix her. Why did she die?
             And wherefore could I not save her by tricks?

If I had greater strength, death would run dry.

PADMÉ   There's aught within our massive galaxy

That naught can fix, no matter what we do.   75

Omnipotent thou art not, canst thou see?

ANAKIN   Yet should I be! And will be someday, true.

Most powerful among the Jedi yet:

This shall I be: it is mine earnest vow.

One day I shall the strength of death offset.   80

PADMÉ   O, Anakin, such fury in thy brow.

ANAKIN   'Tis Obi-Wan who is to blame, indeed:

In him's the green-eyed monster, jealousy.

He holds me back, so I may not succeed!

PADMÉ   What are these words? Pray speak, what troubles

thee?   85

ANAKIN   These hands, O, wretched hands that took enjoyment

In killing Tusken men an 'twere child's play.

Yet, O, they did make love to this employment;

They are not near my conscience: never, nay.

The men, though, could not hope to satisfy   90

My sick bloodthirsty soul, which needed more.

So kill'd I all—the women, children, aye,

I bath'd the lot of them in filth and gore.

They are like animals fit for a feast,

And I did bring to slaughter ev'ry one.   95

My soul doth fester like a raging beast,

From hate to greater hate mine heart doth run.

PADMÉ   Thine anger is but human, Anakin.

ANAKIN   I am a Jedi, and should better be.

PADMÉ   My spirit is to thine a joinèd twin,   100

Thus may I bear thine ev'ry agony.

Enter R2-D2 *and* C-3PO.

R2-D2	Beep, meep, beep, squeak.
PADMÉ	—R2, I pray, what is't?
R2-D2	Meep, whistle, hoo!
C-3PO	—He doth report this news:

Some message comes from Obi-Wan Kenobi,
A name most unfamiliar unto me.   105
Good Master Anakin, know you this name?

ANAKIN   [*aside:*] Midst all these moments of defeating grief
I have almost my senses quite forgot.
Good Master Obi-Wan, I'll heed your call.
[*To R2-D2:*] Good droid, the message thou shalt
                                                   play anon.   110

R2-D2 *begins playing the message. Enter* OBI-WAN KENOBI *aside,
in beam. Enter* YODA *and* MACE WINDU *on balcony, hearing the
message as well.*

OBI-WAN   My long-range transmitter hath been destroy'd.
Deliver this dispatch to Coruscant.

I've track'd the bounty hunter, Jango Fett,
To Geonosis and its foundries vast,
Constructing battle droids by night and day.   11:
The vile Trade Federation now doth scheme
To join its great droid army unto these.
'Tis clear that Viceroy Gunray hath conspir'd
The senator, e'en Amidala, to
Assassinate. The Corporate Alliance,   120
Together with the Commerce Guilds, have pledg'd
Allegiance—aye, and armies—to Count Dooku.
They form e'en now a . . . Wait, I am attack'd!
[Exit Obi-Wan from beam, brandishing his lightsaber.

YODA   More hath taken place
                On Geonosis, I feel,   12:
                Than reveal'd hath been.

MACE   Yea, Master, I agree. Brave Anakin,
                Let us avengers to Count Dooku be.
                Thou must remain where presently thou art,
                The senator, at all costs, to protect.   130
                This is mine order, thy priority.

ANAKIN   I understand, my master, and obey.
                                [Exeunt Yoda and Mace from balcony.
                                    Exeunt R2-D2 and C-3PO.

PADMÉ   They never shall reach Obi-Wan in time,
                'Tis halfway 'cross the galaxy immense.
                Behold, for I do speak with reason's rhyme,   13:
                Yon Geonosis is but parsecs hence.

ANAKIN   'Tis true, if e'en the man is still alive.

PADMÉ   What cause hast thou to speak with bitter words?
                Thou wouldst not stay and him thine help deprive.
                He is thy mentor, you are like two birds   14(
                Who fly together t'ward a common thing.

ANAKIN   Forsooth, the man is like a father gull,
                Who rais'd his fledgling till it could take wing,
                He shar'd his nest with me, my faults did cull,
                And, with paternal love, taught me to fly.   145
                I know the duty I do owe to him,
                Yet thou heard'st Master Windu's strict reply:
                I must stay here, not fly upon a whim.

PADMÉ   His order was to guard me, not to hide,
                And I shall soar to help thine Obi-Wan.   150
                If thou shalt some protection yet provide,
                Thou must come with me till mine errand's done.

ANAKIN   O, wondrous wit of women's strength thou hast,
                And I am all entangl'd in thy braid.
                We shall find Obi-Wan, and at the last   155
                The Jedi Council's orders are obey'd.

          Enter R2-D2 *and* C-3PO *as all enter the cruiser.*

C-3PO   Now unto space we fly—it works me woe:
                Methought that I would never travel so.

                                              [*Exeunt.*

                    SCENE 3.
                On the planet Coruscant.

                Enter JEDI 1 *and* JEDI 2.

JEDI 1   Good friend, well met.
JEDI 2   —And thee as well, holla!
                How hast thou spent this lovely, merry day?

JEDI 1	A'wondering o'er what the future brings.
JEDI 2	Indeed? What is it that thou wonderest?
JEDI 1	Our stories and our strivings and our wars:
	Shall they in other times remember'd be?
	Is't possible, that some long time from now,
	Mayhap in galaxy far, far away,
	Our tales shall be imparted to the young?
	Will there be anyone who doth recall 10
	Wise Master Yoda's striking witticisms,
	Or noble Master Windu's boundless might?
	What would some future, far-off galaxy
	Think of our battles and adventures here?
	Shall our Republic yet remember'd be 1
	When all empirically is past and gone?
JEDI 2	O, heavy thoughts! Pray, let me rest thy mind,
	For I have often wonder'd this myself.
JEDI 1	Yea, truly? What conclusions hast thou reach'd?
JEDI 2	But this: why should another galaxy 2
	Well in the future e'er have need of us?
	The future of another place shall be
	Far different than we could ever think.
	Canst thou imagine folk in some far place
	All gather'd round to see our stories play'd— 2
	Their young men in our clothing all attir'd,
	Their women as our princesses array'd,
	Their builders fashioning a scene to match,
	Their artisans detailing starship parts,
	Their scholars indexing each term of ours, 30
	Their engineers attempting to make droids,
	Their foolish jesters mashing up our words?
	'Tis near unthinkable, some culture hence

	That knows of our beloved, sacred Force.	
JEDI 1	My friend, thy words are unexpected balm.	35
	Long time ahead in galaxy far off,	
	They shall have situations hard enough	
	That they need not rehearse our troubl'd times.	
JEDI 2	Thou seest? 'Tis plain. Unless our stories were	
	Some maudlin form of entertainment. Ha!	40
JEDI 1	How passing strange such galaxy would be.	
JEDI 2	And now to supper. Wilt thou come?	
JEDI 1	—Lead on!	

[Exeunt Jedi 1 and Jedi 2.

Enter CHANCELLOR PALPATINE.

PALPATINE	The actors are arrang'd, the scene is set,	
	The script itself is written in Fate's hand.	
	Still, some few wisps of drama must unfold	45
	Ere I do rise beyond this theatre.	
	The witless players make approach anon,	
	Some have their lines prewritten in mine hand,	
	For I have paid them well to act my play.	
	The others are mere tools unto my will,	50
	Not players they, but play'd by my deceits.	
	Mine entrance through the portico unto	
	The stage that Fortune hath design'd for me	
	Is imminent, the role for which I live.	
	My Senate role was merely cameo,	55
	And chancellor is merely understudy	
	Unto that part I cherish: emperor.	
	Now grasp it swiftly, worthy Palpatine:	
	Make sure the entrances and exits are	

   Directed to the purpose of thine act.   60
   From groundling unto stalls and balcony
   The globe itself is thine, if thou so choose.

Enter YODA, MACE WINDU, BAIL ORGANA, JAR JAR BINKS, SENATOR
  ASK AAK, *and* VICE CHANCELLOR MAS AMEDDA.

BAIL   'Tis clear the Commerce Guilds prepare for war,
     Of that we are beyond all doubt by now.

PALPATINE Count Dooku hath devis'd a treaty with 65
     The Guilds, that much is sure.

ASK   —Debate no more!
     The army of the clones must soon be ours.
     'Tis ready for the taking—we would be
     But folly-fallen fools to pass it by.

BAIL   Nay, our debate is neither clos'd nor done. 70
     The Senate never shall approve the use
     Of clones unless the sep'ratists attack.

MAS   This crisis doth demand such measures as
     Would not elsewise be us'd. The Senate must
     Convey what powers to the chancellor 75
     We may, to stifle this emergency.
     He then may, by supreme command, approve
     Creation of an army of the clones.

PALPATINE What senator would have such courage to
     Propose such radical amendment, eh? 80

MAS   If Amidala were but here.

PALPATINE   —Indeed.

         [Exeunt all but Jar Jar.

JAR JAR Insinuation fills my troubl'd ears—
     'Tis clear this senator and Palpatine

Wish me to act the part of Padmé here
And vote the chancellor a pow'r complete.   85
They would play me as though I were a pipe,
With stops and whistles made for their employ.
They would pluck out the heart of my myst'ry,
Would sound me from my lowest note unto
The top of my compass if they had th'skill.   90
I shall not be so play'd, for I am not
The fool for which they take me, here to be
Conducted in a ballad dissonant.
Yet of mine own accord, I see this path:
Mine efforts—since the Jedi first did come   95
To my Naboo—have been t'ward harmony,
Betwixt the Gugans and Naboo at first,
And then, in Coruscant, t'ward peace profound
For ev'ry race within our galaxy.
I have not power to foresee how all   100
These matters shall unfold. Still, conscience doth
Compel me to continue as I may,
And strive for reconciliation e'er.
Methinks these sep'ratists are rank and vile,
E'er striving to create division harsh.   105
Our dear Republic, though imperfect 'tis,
Is still the galaxy's profoundest hope
For peace among the races that exist.
Mayhap an army to protect our aims
Shall be the best solution. O, that I   110
Could have some knowledge of the future time.
Yet lacking knowledge thus, I only know
That which, o'er time, hath been made known to me,
And judging thus, I do trust Palpatine

And shall support his labors to protect   11
Th'Republic, even by an army here.
Go confidently to the Senate, Binks,
There shall I aid the common good, methinks.

                                                    [*Exit.*

SCENE 4.

On the planet Geonosis.

Enter OBI-WAN KENOBI, *bound in fetters, and* COUNT DOOKU.

OBI-WAN   O, traitor vile! You wretched, scheming rogue.
DOOKU   You have it wrong, my friend. What we have here
            Is but a failure to communicate.
            My strong associates have gone too far,
            To see you bound is madness to mine eyes.
OBI-WAN   Yet 'tis your cool hand that leads here, 'tis true?
DOOKU   'Tis naught to do with me, believe me, sir.
            I shall petition for your quick release.
OBI-WAN   I hope it shall not be too long a time,
            For I've important work to do hereon.   10
DOOKU   Well said, and to the point: say, wherefore hath
            A Jedi Knight to Geonosis come?
OBI-WAN   I track a bounty hunter, Jango Fett.
            Know you the man?
DOOKU   —No bounty hunters live
            Herein of which I am aware, because   15
            The Geonosians do not trust their kind.
OBI-WAN   Yea, who would blame them for this sound mistrust?
            Yet he is here, of that I am convinc'd.

DOOKU   'Tis piteous our paths did never cross
           Ere now, brave Obi-Wan, for Qui-Gon e'er   20
           Spoke well of you. Would that he still did live,
           For in this time his counsel would prove true.

OBI-WAN   Nay, Qui-Gon Jinn would never join with you.

DOOKU   Be not so sure, young Jedi, all may not
           Be quite so clear as you imagine 'tis.   25
           You do forget, perhaps, that he was once
           Apprentic'd unto me as you to him.
           The Senate's rank corruption was well known
           To him, and ne'er would he have walk'd their path
           If he had learn'd the truth of where it leads.   30

OBI-WAN   What truth?

DOOKU   —A truth you never shall believe.
           Pray, listen with an open, willing ear.
           I shall unveil to you a wondrous tale,
           How the Republic hath been undermin'd
           And is, e'en now, within the full control   35
           Of one most fear'd, the dark lord of the Sith.

OBI-WAN   Such tales are meant to frighten children, Count,
           Yet are but fiction in the light of day.
           The Jedi would be well aware of such
           A power, were it making some ascent.   40

DOOKU   The dark side of the Force doth make them blind.
           Full many senators, e'en hundreds, aye,
           Are rul'd by the Sith lord, Darth Sidious.

OBI-WAN   Your words are but an idle tale, sir.

DOOKU   The Federation viceroy once did work   45
           Darth Sidious withal, but was betray'd
           A decade since by this dark, evil lord.
           The viceroy came to me and told me all.

I prithee, join with me, strong Obi-Wan.
When our strength is combin'd, we shall conclude   50
This bitter conflict and bring order to
The galaxy entire.

OBI-WAN   —I never shall
Join with you; I would rather be destroy'd.

DOOKU   Your liberation may prove difficult.

                         [Exit Obi-Wan.

I tell him naught but truth, yet he is deaf: 55
These Jedi are made weak by their own pride.
Reality shall come a'crashing in
Unless the Jedi ope their eyes anon.
Still, I would haply have been join'd by him,
Together he and I could rule as Sith.   60
Zounds! Mine ambition knows no end, 'tis true—
E'en as I serve my lord, I seek his place.
Ha! Obi-Wan's defiance matters not,
Reduc'd to bones he shall be by our plot.

                              [Exit.

SCENE 5.

On the planet Coruscant, inside the Senate chamber.

Enter CHANCELLOR PALPATINE, VICE CHANCELLOR MAS AMEDDA, JAR JAR BINKS, *and other* MEMBERS OF THE GALACTIC SENATE. *Enter* YODA *and* MACE WINDU *on balcony, observing the proceedings.*

JAR JAR   'Tis clear dat desa sep'ratist, dey
Did make a pact wid Federation.
Ye senators, dellow felagates,

	We should respond to dis big threatee	
	To our Republic wid a big show:	5
	So meesa do propose de Senate	
	Immediate emergency pow'r	
	Give to de Chancellor Supreme, yea?	
SENATORS	'Tis Palpatine, aye, Palatine, hurrah!	
MAS	Give order in the Senate, order now!	10
PALPATINE	It is with a reluctance limitless	

PALPATINE It is with a reluctance limitless
That I receive and do accept this charge.
Democracy is that which I do love,
And our Republic is mine heart's desire.
I shall lay down this burthen of vast pow'r   15
When time shall be this crisis hath declin'd.
My first act, by this fresh authority,
Shall be a mighty army to establish,
Which shall protect and serve th'Republic's cause
And counter this increasing, ugly threat   20
That cometh from the faithless sep'ratists.

SENATORS An army, aye! For Palpatine, hurrah!

MACE [to Yoda:] Then it is done, the army shall exist:
Republic hath a loaded weapon gain'd.
The Jedi who remain shall come with me   25
To Geonosis, aiding Obi-Wan.

YODA Visit I shall make
To cloners on Kamino.
Their story I'll hear.

There shall I inspect   30
This clone army, and lay claim
In Republic's name.

                                        [Exeunt.

ACT
V

SCENE 1.

On the planet Geonosis, the droid foundry and the execution arena.

Enter ANAKIN SKYWALKER *and* PADMÉ,
in ship with C-3PO *and* R2-D2.

PADMÉ   Dost see the posts of steam that yonder rise?
               They tell of some exhaust ports down below.

ANAKIN   Well seen, my lady, keen are thy two eyes.
               Therein shall I touch down, to meet our foe.

PADMÉ   I prithee, Anakin, whate'er befalls
               Take thou instruction from mine ev'ry move,
               Should tact and manners fail inside these walls
               War follows if our rivals disapprove.
               I, as a member of the Senate strong,
               Belike may find a diplomatic end   10
               To all this conflict and its senseless wrong.

ANAKIN   Aye, thy look doth all arguments suspend.
                         [*Exeunt Anakin and Padmé, disembarking.*

R2-D2   [*aside:*] Shall I remain to let them suffer ill?
               Forbid it so! They'll have my droidly help.
               [*To C-3PO:*] Beep, meep, squeak, beep!

C-3PO   —Mine errant, impish friend,   1
               If they had needed our assistance, then
               'Tis plain they need but merely ask for it.
               Thou couldst much learn about the human mind,
               If thou by me wouldst be instructed.

R2-D2   —Squeak!

Enter ANAKIN SKYWALKER *and* PADMÉ, *on balcony.*

ANAKIN   A large facility, with many routes,   20
              I wonder where we shall find Obi-Wan.
PADMÉ   Such wayward paths do trail these harsh disputes
              And lead us unto webs by darkness spun.
                                    [Exeunt Anakin and Padmé.
R2-D2   Meep, beep, meep, whistle, beep, squeak, whistle, hoo!
C-3PO   For a mechanic, thinkest thou too much!   25
R2-D2   Beep, whistle, squeak, meep, hoo!
C-3PO   —I programm'd am
              To understand humanity and all
              Its complex, varied moods and attitudes.
              O, what a piece of work's humanity—
              How infinite in faculty! In form   30
              And moving, how express and admirable!
              Presume thou not to doubt mine expertise.
R2-D2   Squeak, whistle, squeak, beep, hoo, beep, whistle,
                                                      squeak!
C-3PO   "What doth that mean?" thou sayest, naught droid!
              The plain conclusion's this: I am in charge.   35
R2-D2   [*aside:*] I have a nobler, more important charge:
              These humans to protect, as best I may.
              [*To C-3PO:*] Meep, hoo!
C-3PO   —O wither goest thou, small rogue?
              Thou knowest not what lies beyond, R2!
              Hast thou lost ev'ry ounce of common sense?   40
                        [R2-D2 disembarks with C-3PO in pursuit.
              Alack! If thou shalt go, then wait for me!
              Is't possible thou knowest where thou lead'st?

Enter ANAKIN SKYWALKER *and* PADMÉ, *pursued by* GEONOSIANS.

ANAKIN   You brutes, taste my lightsaber's hostile touch!
                          [Anakin slays several Geonosians, who flee,
                                      passing by C-3PO and R2-D2.

C-3PO   You beasts, depart from us at once! O! O!
                          [Anakin and Padmé reach a precipice
                                      above the droid foundry.

PADMÉ   Our path doth lead from trouble unto trouble: 4.
                Behold, our way doth cease upon this ledge.

ANAKIN   The plank, indeed, our misery doth double,
                For now it disappears, 'tis but a wedge!

PADMÉ   I fall!
                          [Padmé falls, landing on the conveyor belt below.

ANAKIN   —My love, my life, I follow thee!
                          [Anakin jumps to the conveyor belt.

Enter GEONOSIANS, *fighting* ANAKIN. *He destroys them.*

PADMÉ   A vast machine with plates and hammer'd steel—   5(
                One wayward step shall be the death of me.
                If I but guide my steps with even keel,
                Then peradventure I may best it yet.
                Be swift, my feet, the mallets to avoid!
                          [She runs underneath several large hammering
                                      and clamping devices, escaping their blows.
                'Tis like a gauntlet by some devil set: 55
                Is this the scene in which I am destroy'd?

ANAKIN   My Jedi senses aid my progress here,
                Though still mine heart, my Padmé is far gone!
                Her death herein—O, 'tis mine utmost fear:
                I need no stronger reason to press on!   6(

                [C-3PO and R2-D2 arrive on the
                precipice above the droid foundry.

C-3PO   O, madness most profound, what sight is this?
           Yea, shut me off—machines that make machines!
           Such strange perversity I never saw.

R2-D2   Beep, meep.

               [R2-D2 bumps into C-3PO from behind.

C-3PO   —Take care, R2, I almost fell!

R2-D2   *[aside:]* Adventure shall befall him, ere he knows!   65
           [To C-3PO:] Meep, whistle, hoo!

              [R2-D2 bumps into C-3PO, knocking him
              off the precipice onto a passing foundry vehicle.

C-3PO   —I fall! Aye, ask for me
           Tomorrow, you shall find me a scrap droid!
           A nightmare, this! We're not in Tatooine,
           Not anymore: O, there's no place like home!

             [The vehicle drops C-3PO onto a conveyor belt.
           Have I no heart, that I this pain deserve?   70

              [R2-D2 fires his boosters and flies
              into the foundry chamber.

R2-D2   *[aside:]* I fly, my friends to save! Beep, whistle, hoo!

              [A Geonosian attacks Padmé.

PADMÉ   O, nasty, wretched creature, let me go!
           Alas, I fall into some larger container.
           Such unforgiving strife doth work us woe,
           That our hopes have turn'd grim could not be plainer. 75

              [The large bucket into which Padmé falls is
              swept away by a machine.

C-3PO   I wonder what became of poor R2,
           Who doth excel at finding trouble. Ah!

             [C-3PO's head is removed and replaced
              with a battle droid head.

I've lost mine head or, rather, body too!
I know not which—for where doth sense reside?
Mine eyes still see the foundry, yet themselves   8(
Have not the pow'r to move, and still my feet
Do feel the ground, yet have no pow'r to think!
O, senseless life, when head and trunk are riv'n
In twain, when body is from brain detach'd!

> [The machine attaches a battle droid body
> to C-3PO's head, resulting in C-3PO 1—
> C-3PO's body with a battle droid head—
> and C-3PO 2, C-3PO's head with
> a battle droid body.

C-3PO 1   My body's fix'd unto another droid!   8

C-3PO 2   Mine head another body hath assum'd—
Confusion bleak that splits my soul in two!

> [Exeunt C-3PO 1 and C-3PO 2.

ANAKIN   The Force is with me here, these beasts to fight:
Yet they are more than even I can stand!

> [Anakin falls, and his hand is
> clamped beneath a steel plate.

I fall—the fiends o'ercome this Jedi Knight!   9(
O, shall I finish'd be by mine own hand?

PADMÉ   This massive barrel shall undo me quite,
For it shall soon with molten lead be fill'd.
O, this shall be a terrifying sight:
A senator outdone by liquid spill'd.   9:

R2-D2   [aside:] Now to it, droid, and do thy fleetest work,
Connect with the machine to make it stop.

> [R2-D2 plugs into the machine and stops the
> molten metal from filling Padmé's barrel. The barrel
> is released and falls. Exit R2-D2.

PADMÉ   Sav'd from the heat, but still I'm in the fire:
               I fall, and shall some knocks receive, sans doubt.
               The barrel crashes—fie!—occasion dire!   100
               Now helplessly, like water, I'm pour'd out.

ANAKIN   The blades upon this belt shall be mine end—
               A Jedi split upon a razor's slice—
               Unless I may mine energies expend
               And beat this apparatus in a trice.   105

               [Anakin dodges swiftly as a machine
               cuts his hand free from the steel plate;
               his lightsaber is destroyed in the process.

               My freedom, aye, but not without a cost:
               My new lightsaber hath been made unfit.
               When we find Obi-Wan, who now is lost,
               I'll face odd quirks and remnants of his wit.

               Enter JANGO FETT *and several* DROIDEKAS,
                  as GEONOSIANS *surround* PADMÉ.

JANGO   I promise, move once and it shall be your last, Jedi.   110
               You, droidekas, take him away!

                                        [Jango Fett moves aside.

PADMÉ   *[aside:]* Our journey to find Obi-Wan is o'er,
               For sure we're o'ercome by bitter foes,
               The vile assassins who did try before
               To end my life may now their death impose.   115
               Aye, truly, it doth seem I make my walk
               Unto some tragic and untimely end.
               Yet, just as heart should fear and mind should balk,
               I fear it not, because love doth suspend
               The fear that otherwise would fill my soul.   120

Indeed, e'en as death looms before mine eyes
Mine heart is by another one made whole:
What I had spurn'd, I now shall recognize.
The battle we have lost, but not the war:
E'en if we die, our love shall have its day.   12.

ANAKIN   Be not afraid, O, lady I adore.

PADMÉ   To die is not what brings mine heart dismay,
For verily mine heart doth daily burn—
A piece of a death arrives with each new sun—
Since thou into my life hast made return.   13(

ANAKIN   What mean'st thou, to what end do thy words run?

PADMÉ   The thing mine heart doth realize at last.
Although it comes too late, do thou hear me:
I love thee, Anakin.

ANAKIN   —Elation vast!
Yet I had thought our love was not to be: 13.
The moment was not right, our love to bloom,
For truly it would mean a life of lies,
Thus bringing to our lives a world of doom.
These were your words, which from your lips did rise.

PADMÉ   The situation dooming us therein   14(
Seems less important since I've found my bliss.
I truly, deeply love thee, Anakin.

ANAKIN   Then if we die, we die upon a kiss.

                    [They kiss as they are led, guarded,
                        into the execution arena.

Enter OBI-WAN KENOBI, bound against a pillar, and cheering
SPECTATORS. Enter COUNT DOOKU, JANGO FETT, POGGLE THE LESSER,
NUTE GUNRAY, and BOBA FETT on balcony, surveying the scene.

OBI-WAN   My Padawan hath come to save my life—

	Mayhap his action doth misguided seem,	145
	Since he and Padmé both arrive in bonds.	
	Yet I confess their presence is most welcome.	
	For two shall make a stronger stand than one,	
	And three shall make a stronger stand than two.	
PADMÉ	A clip for holding hair I shall conceal.	150
	Though normally it keeps mine hair aright,	
	Here shall it yet another purpose serve	
	And keep my fate aright. Now hide, sly clip.	

                  [Padmé hides the clip in her mouth.
                  She and Anakin are chained to pillars.

OBI-WAN	Fair greetings, eager, faithful Padawan.	
	I had begun to wonder if, indeed,	155
	The message that I sent had been receiv'd.	
ANAKIN	I did, and retransmitted as you said.	
	'Twas all as you did order, Master, yea,	
	Until we did decide to rescue you.	
OBI-WAN	Thy plan was brave, though Fate had other plans.	160
	And now your fate is bound with mine, in chains.	
	[*Aside:*] Why do I prick at him, when he but tried	
	To serve me a good turn? More thanks he doth	
	Deserve than this, though his work was in vain.	
POGGLE	[*to spectators:*] I prithee, viewers all, maintain the peace.	165
	The executions shall commence anon!	
SPECTATORS	Huzzah!	

Enter into the arena three beasts—the ACKLAY, *the* NEXU,
and the REEK—*and* THEIR KEEPERS.

OBI-WAN	—From bad to worse—what monstrous beasts!
REEK	E'en now are we three met again,
	I—thunder, lighting—bring my pain.

ACKLAY	Yea, when the hurlyburly's done,	170
	A meal we shall have lost or won.	
NEXU	That will be ere the set of sun.	
REEK	But where the place?	
ACKLAY	—E'en here is fine.	
NEXU	Aye, here upon these folk to dine.	
REEK	I come, the reek, with horns severe,	175
	A coat of armor, sharp as spear,	
	Such bulk as could destroy a ship,	
	No creature from my grasp may slip.	
ACKLAY	The acklay I, with teeth like knives,	
	Made for defeating human lives.	180
	Six legs, like iron set with spikes,	
	I rage and I do as I likes.	
NEXU	I am the nexu, small but fierce,	
	With claws design'd frail flesh to pierce.	
	Barbs on my back to work you woe,	185
	I'll catch ye whether swift or slow.	

BEASTS   Now foes are food, and food is fair,
                Come, blood, through fog and filthy air.
                  [The beasts approach Obi-Wan, Anakin, and Padmé.

ANAKIN   I have a feeling bad about this, sir.
                        [Padmé releases one of her bonds with the
                      hidden hair clip and climbs to the top of her pillar.

PADMÉ   Whilst my two friends do gape and wonder so,   190
                Already liberty have I secur'd.

OBI-WAN   Remain thou calm, young Padawan, relax
                And concentrate upon the moment.

ANAKIN   —Aye,
                But what of Padmé, tender, sweet, and true?

OBI-WAN   It doth appear she's ris'n above her fear.   195

ANAKIN   Behold, my clever lady stands atop
                The pillar, there the creatures to o'erthrow.

OBI-WAN   Here come the beasts: 'tis either them or us.
                        [The acklay approaches Obi-Wan,
                              slashing its pincers at him.

ACKLAY   This one is mine, shall be my feast,
                I strike at him, my rage releas'd.   200
                O, he is quick and parries me,
                Alas, I've hit his chains, he's free!

OBI-WAN   Shalt thou not make a hardier attempt?
                To think that I was e'er of thee afeard.
                        [The acklay and Obi-Wan continue to
                              skirmish as the reek charges toward Anakin.

REEK   I'll ram the other one anon,   205
                And show him all the reek's vast brawn.
                I'll double all his toil and trouble,
                Until he burns like cauldron bubble.

ANAKIN   This one is not as fearsome as he seems—

O'erleaping him, I land upon his back   21●
Now come, thick chains that bound me to the post,
Around his neck, I'll ride the beastie yet!

          [The nexu approaches Padmé, leaping
              up the pillar on which she perches.

NEXU   The last is mine, and soft her flesh,
               Made for a meal that's ripe and fresh.
               Come down, and fill my belly up,   21.●
               Today on blood-red meat I'll sup!

PADMÉ   Down, wretched beast, with fetters do I strike!
               I'll teach to thee a lesson of Naboo—
               Come once again and I shall pound thy pate.
               O, agony! The beast hath scratch'd my spine!   22●

          [The nexu tears into Padmé's back, and she screams.

NEXU   First blood is mine, ram boldly I,
               Once more the pillar I shall try.

NUTE   Ha, ha! The senator is finish'd soon!

OBI-WAN   Mayhap I should this creature not have mock'd,
               For now he comes with stamina renew'd!   22.●
               I roll and dive, yet fear I that, perchance,
               His legs of six are four beyond my skill.

JANGO   *[to Boba:]* Watch well, my son, and thou shalt see
               how a Jedi becometh little more than a morsel,
               tender and raw.   23●

          [The reek knocks Anakin from its back
             as it continues to charge around the arena.

REEK   I'll not be topp'd, thus says the reek,
               This human's pow'r o'er me is weak,
               I toss him off, and thus he falls,
               And now my hunger loudly calls.

ANAKIN   Alas, unseated by this scaly brute,   23

           And now bedragg'd across the turf most harsh.

NEXU   I come again, the dame to eat,
           And shortly shall she taste defeat,
           Then I shall taste a diff'rent feast:
           Provision rare made for a beast!   240

PADMÉ   Thou hadst thy chance, and took the skin from me,
           But thou shalt not receive a second chance.
           Aye, climb thou higher, nasty, hairy fiend—
           So high thou dost forget how long's the fall.
                [Padmé swings from her perch and kicks the
                nexu, which falls to the ground, whimpering.

NUTE   This wench is not allow'd to struggle thus!   245
DOOKU   Methinks, good Viceroy, rules concern her not.
NEXU   I savor, feisty dame, thine hit—
           Meat's richer when one works for it!

OBI-WAN   This many-legged monster ceaseth not,
           The pillar to which I was lately fix'd   250
           Hath been knock'd over in its wrath severe.
           Yet here, an opportunity arises—
           A Geonosian keeper draws too near.
           Ha, ha! His pointed spear becometh mine!
                [Obi-Wan throws the Geonosian keeper
                toward the acklay, skewering it on the
                Geonosian's spear. Meanwhile, the reek slows
                its charge and stops dragging Anakin.

ANAKIN   The creature slows its charge, so I may rise,   255
           And now I sense a diff'rence in its mien:
           Exhausted by this conflict and these games,
           It may a Jedi's calmer mind obey.
           I prithee, listen, animal of might:
           I do not seek to thee domesticate,   260

      For thou art independent, stout, and stern,
      I only ask to see me as thine equal.
      We two shall ride as one, my gallant steed,
      And give thy brutal masters cause to fear.

REEK   His reason speaks a noble word—   265
      Thus he and I shall make a herd.

          [Anakin mounts the reek.

ANAKIN   He that knows better how to tame a beast,
      Now let him speak; 'tis charity to show.

PADMÉ   These fetters I'll unfetter and be free,
      With both hands loose I shall succeed perforce. 270

NEXU   My third attempt shall be the last,
      Prepare thou to be my repast.

        [Anakin's reek charges at and strikes
              the nexu, killing it.

PADMÉ   O, Anakin, my savior and my love!

ANAKIN   Forgive me, lady, for my sore delay,
      'Twas one or two small matters kept me, dove. 275
      Leap down and share a merry ride, I pray.

       [She jumps down onto the reek, behind
        Anakin, while Obi-Wan brandishes his
           spear against the acklay.

OBI-WAN Thou monster, now we have a fairer right,
      Thou hast thy pincers, aye, and I have mine.

ACKLAY Shall acklay be the only beast
      Who shall today enjoy a feast?   280
      Well, to it, then, and let us fight:
      Your death shall sate mine appetite!

OBI-WAN Thou hast the disadvantage, reckless brute,
      For while thy points are all attach'd to thee,
      My spear shall fly and hit thee 'neath thy plates. 285

                                    [*Obi-Wan throws his spear at the*
                                    acklay, wounding it in the shoulder.

ACKLAY   A simple prick shall not suffice,
              If thou dost needle, in a trice
              I'll match thy stickers quid pro quo
              And watch your blood begin to flow.

OBI-WAN   'Tis good to know when holding maketh sense,   290
              'Tis better yet to know when one should fold,
              'Tis best to know when one should walk away,
              Yet now the time hath come for me to run!
              I'll join the others—yea, no gambler I!

                                    [*Obi-Wan runs and jumps onto*
                                        the reek, behind Padmé.

NUTE   'Tis not the script that I did write for her—   295
              She should be in a monster's gut ere now!
              Pray, Jango, go, and finish her anon!

DOOKU   All patience, Viceroy—she shall surely die.

                        Enter DROIDEKAS.

OBI-WAN   From worse to worst, we are surrounded.
ANAKIN   —Fie!
              Methought our freedom almost was acquir'd.   300

Enter MACE WINDU *on balcony, brandishing his lightsaber against*
JANGO FETT, *as many* JEDI, *including* KI-ADI-MUNDI, *rush into the*
          arena below. GEONOSIANS *flee the arena.*

MACE   Bear witness, old boy, your plot is o'erthrown.
DOOKU   Bold Master Windu, all my gratitude
              I bear to you for joining us herein.

MACE   This produce is pulp; fiction is your plan.
            To put it plain: your reign of terror ends.   305

DOOKU   'Tis brave, yet foolish, mine old Jedi friend.
            You are outnumber'd far beyond your ken.

MACE   I think not. Soon you shall be in a cell,
            Or mayhap dead: it matters not to me.

DOOKU   We shall both see what twists Fate knits for us.   310

Enter a large battalion of BATTLE DROIDS, *including* C-3PO 1
in the ranks, attacking.

JANGO   Inflam'd my passion is—thus may you die in flames,
                                                            Jedi!
            [Jango shoots flames at Mace, who leaps to the stage.

MACE   Behold, how like a kite I do descend—
            I hover on, propell'd by Windu's Force.

OBI-WAN   With hope renew'd we fight this battle grand,
            New lightsabers provided by our friends!   315

C-3PO 1   Alas, I cannot feel my legs aright—
            Mayhap I have a need for maintenance.
                        *[A blast knocks Anakin, Padmé, and
                            Obi-Wan from the reek's back.*

ANAKIN   [*to reek:*] My sturdy mount, I thank thee for thine aid,
            Flee now at once, and hope speed thee away.

REEK   A battle is no place for me,   320
            Thus reek shall turn his tail and flee.
                                            [Exit the reek.

PADMÉ   A chariot doth nearly run me o'er,
            I'll leap in, throw the driver out of joint!
                        *[Padmé leaps onto a passing chariot,
                            subduing its driver and taking the reins.*

ANAKIN   My lady, I shall join thee thereupon

To battle from a better vantage point.   32.

Enter more BATTLE DROIDS, *with* C-3PO 2 *in the ranks.*

C-3PO 2   What is this noise that clatters in mine ears?
    A battle—O, alas, take me therefrom!
    Yet do these legs, these stubborn borrow'd legs
    Propel mine head where I'd not wish to go!
    O, grave mistake—I am not programm'd for   330
    Destruction, nay, but merely etiquette!

C-3PO 1   I shoot, the Jedi vermin to destroy,
    But, O, here comes a shot toward mine head!
        [A ricocheting blaster fire destroys C-3PO 1's
        battle droid head, as his body falls to the ground.

OBI-WAN   We are outnumber'd sorely in this fight!

JANGO   These Jedi are no match for Jango Fett. Feel the fire of   33.
    my blaster, Jedi scum, as your candle I do snuff! Down

below hath Windu fallen—these other Jedi being no
match for me, I'll seek him out and try him in the field.
        [Jango flies to the stage, facing off with Mace.

Enter the REEK, *charging at* JANGO FETT.

REEK   The reek doth charge again, my friends,
            And for my rage I'll make amends.   340
            Charge at this one who works you woe,
            That he may feel the reek's harsh blow.
JANGO   'Sblood, this beast doth run o'er me as one with the
            strength of a hundred bulls! Now doth it mean to charge
            on me again. Thou may'st have knock'd me down once,   345
            monster, yet no one hath e'er twice brought me defeat.
                        [Jango fires at the reek, killing it.
MACE   Unjustly done, the noble steed to slay!
            Now thou shalt die hard; with a vengeance comes
            Mace Windu boldly—lay on, Jango Fett!
JANGO   How quick he comes, with speed both vast and harsh.   350
            Mine ev'ry shot he doth avoid, as though I were but a
            child's plaything to him. E'en closer now, and closer—fie!
            This is the end, aye, here falleth the Fett.
                       [Mace cuts off Jango's head and
                             then looks to Count Dooku.
DOOKU   My bounty hunter quite undone. Methinks
            This may portend the changing of the tide   355
            Of battle. See how Master Windu doth
            Behold me with his eyes of burnish'd steel.
BOBA   Behold I this foul scene with the eyes of a child.
            Must I now grow into a man at once? My father,
            cruelly murder'd by this Jedi. Remember this moment,   360

Boba, and let it mark thine ev'ry footstep forward.
My father shall be aveng'd, and I, in time, shall take
his place as the most vicious bounty hunter that e'er
did roam the galaxy. Learn this lesson, Jedi: like the
wild, unruly hydra, you cannot strike the head from   365
the Fetts but another shall grow in its place.

                                     [Exit Boba.

C-3PO 2   Die, Jedi dogs! Alas, what did I say?
I am so sorry for my body's actions,
This is beyond all proper protocol!

               [A Jedi uses the Force to knock down
                C-3PO 2, and another battle droid falls
                           slain on top of him.

Beg pardon, I am trapp'd. Might someone help?   370
PADMÉ   Our chariot's destroy'd but we fight on,
Belike the battle turns toward our gain.

ANAKIN   Our adversaries may soon be withdrawn:
Perchance our struggle hath not been in vain.
But justify thy words, belovèd, please: 375
Is this thy "diplomatic end," I ask?

PADMÉ   "Determinèd negotiations," these!

Thy words were better suited for this task.

        [The acklay approaches Obi-Wan from
                    behind, unbeknownst to him.

OBI-WAN   I fight these battle droids, and now they flee—

          What fear doth shake them? Certainly, not I?   380

ACKLAY   Here is the one who did me wrong,

          Who prick'd me with a bitter prong.

          Yet I shall do him better still:

          His life or mine, aye, come what will!

OBI-WAN   The beast hath come again to pay his debts!   385

          But little doth he know my newfound strength:

          When he did seek to slay me earlier,

          I had no lightsaber and was not whole.

          Taste thou the flaming touch of Jedi's sword!

          I'll take these legs one at a time from thee,   390

          Sweep underneath and cut thee down to size!

        [Obi-Wan runs under the acklay, cutting off
          its legs as he goes, and then runs it through.

ACKLAY   A bitter pain, a monster's trick,

          He injureth me to the quick.

          The acklay's life shall be no more,

          He triumphs where none hath before.   395

                      [The acklay dies.

           Enter R2-D2.

R2-D2   *[aside:]* The battle is laid out on ev'ry side,

          As Jedi strong with battle droids conflict.

          How wide the skirmish, yet may I, a droid,

          Pass safely through for none think me a threat.

          How may I render service to my friends?   400

Ah, there is my companion, Threepio,
Upended on the field, awaiting aid.
Since I did bring C-3PO to this,
'Tis meet that I remove him from it, too.
                              [R2-D2 approaches C-3PO 2.
[To C-3PO 2:] Beep, meep!

C-3PO 2   —O, R2, wherefore art thou here? 405

R2-D2   Meep, whistle, squeak!

C-3PO 2   —What art thou doing, droid?
                    [R2-D2 releases a magnet and attaches it to
                       C-3PO 2's head, removing the head from
                                     the battle droid body.
             Cease this at once, thou shalt my circuits strain.
             My neck—alack! Once more my body's gone.
             At least this time I have not lost mine head!
             Where shalt thou take me, dragging me along?   410

R2-D2   Beep, whistle, meep, beep, hoo, meep, whistle, nee!
                       [R2-D2 pulls C-3PO 2's head next to
                          C-3PO 1's body, joining them once more.

C-3PO   Was e'er a droid beside himself as I?
             Take thou good care, R2, as thou fix'st me!
             I would not scorchèd be by thy repairs.
             'Tis better, aye, yet is mine head aright?   415

OBI-WAN   The battle presses in, and we are ta'en!
             There are too many of them to succeed.

ANAKIN   You are correct, good Master, for our plight
             Looks dismal by the light of droidly fire.

MACE   The deep blue sea hath not such magnitude   420
             As all these battle droids, which come sans end.

DOOKU   By my command, I end this gross attack.
             Cease droids, that I may speak unto the Jedi.

                    [*The battle droids draw up their
                        weapons and stop approaching.*

          Brash Master Windu, gallantly you've fought,
          And shall one day remember'd be within   425
          The Jedi archives' thorough history.
          Yet now the battle's finish'd. Make surrender,
          And you may spare your humble, little lives.
MACE   We Jedi Knights shall ne'er be subject to
          The sad, false law and order you would bring,   430
          And neither shall we serve as hostages.
          We are not coins with which you may acquire
          A vast Republic. Nay, Count Dooku, ne'er.
DOOKU   You have bought mine apologies, old friend,
          And purchas'd in the deal your own quick deaths.   435
PADMÉ   Behold, above—how many ships do come!

          Enter YODA *with ships full of* CLONE TROOPERS.
                Enter RUMOR *severally.*

RUMOR   Forsooth, full many ships fly on the scene,
          O'er all the heads of the combatants here.
          Resounding, like the noise of a machine,
          Surrounding all, they bring both hope and fear.   440
          O'er all the clones doth Yoda take the lead,
          On deck he standeth, ready for the fight.
          The ships of clones do meet the Jedi need:
          Here strike they now the battle droids with might.
          Confusion in your mind mayhap doth rise: 445
          O, how sly Rumor tangles up your mind!
          Naught knew Count Dooku of the clone surprise,
          For he believ'd they were to him assign'd.

Until good Obi-Wan Kamino found,
Sith plann'd to use the clones as their own force.   450
Instead, the Jedi did these plans confound—
Or so it seems, yet Rumor hath her course.
Now you may think the Jedi have a strength
Above whatever foes they e'er have fac'd.
But do remember that the clones, at length,   455
On the Republic's rolls shall soon be plac'd.
Use your imagination: if the Sith
Nigh run th'Republic, e'en as Dooku said,
Disaster to the Jedi comes forthwith:
Soon this clone army shall by Sith be led.   460
Here to the Jedi comes, all unforeseen,
Events that shall undo them through and through.
Result shall be a hapless closing scene:
E'en Jedi can't escape a Rumor true.

                                        [*Exit Rumor.*

YODA   [*to troopers:*] Around our allies,   46.
              Those who have surviv'd thus far,
              A margin create.

OBI-WAN   These blessèd ships unto our rescue come!
              Behold how with a shocking potency
              They blast the enemy to kingdom come.   47(
              I find myself imbued with gratitude
              For their most sudden advent on the scene.
              The strength they bring is vast and measureless—
              Perhaps could conquer galaxies entire.
              What would befall were they not on our side?   47.
              I hope I ne'er shall witness such a day.

PADMÉ   Make haste, good Jedi all, for we must flee.

ANAKIN   Unto the ships we go—we fly anon!

DOOKU   This interruption's unexpected, aye,
               Yet may still run unto our broader purpose.   480
                         [Exeunt Count Dooku, Nute Gunray,
                              and Poggle the Lesser from balcony.

YODA   If Dooku escapes,
               Rally ever more systems
               To his cause he shall!
                         [Exeunt combatants from the field. The ships
                              holding clone troopers fly away, including a ship
                                   containing Yoda, Mace, Ki-Adi, and other Jedi
                         and another ship containing Obi-Wan, Anakin, and
                              Padmé. Only C-3PO and R2-D2 remain onstage.

C-3PO   Have they all stolen hence, left me asleep?
               R2, I've had a most rare vision, yea: 485
               I've had a dream, past wit of droid to say
               What dream it was: aye, I were but an akk,
               If I did go about t'expound this dream.
               Methought I was—yet no droid can tell what.
               Methought I was—and too, methought I had—   490
               But I am but a patchèd fool, if I
               Will offer to say what methought I had.
               The eyes of droids have never heard, the ears
               Of droids have never seen, droids' circuitry
               Not able been to sense, nor programming   495
               Conceive, nor e'en droids' core to make report,
               What my dream was. I'll speak no more of it.

R2-D2   [aside:] It seems the droid hath bottom'd out his sense.
               Fear not, C-3PO, I'll guide thee hence.
                                             [Exeunt.

SCENE 2.

On the planet Geonosis.

Enter YODA *with* CLONE TROOPERS 1 *and* 2.

TROOPER 1   Small Master Yoda, hear my meek report:
             All forward sites are making their advances.

YODA   Forsooth, very good.
             I shall unto the center
             Of command make way.   5

             Pray, concentrate fire
             On the starship nearest by.
             Thus succeed shall we.

TROOPER 1   Indeed, good Master Jedi. [*To Trooper 2:*] Now, sirrah,
             Move quadrants all to sector five fifteen.   10

                                 [*Exeunt.*

Enter OBI-WAN KENOBI, ANAKIN SKYWALKER, PADMÉ, *and*
      CLONE TROOPERS 3 *and* 4 *on balcony, in ship.*

OBI-WAN   Take care, good friends, and hold fast to the ship.

ANAKIN   [*to Trooper 3:*] Aim just above the fuel cells, so we may
             Destroy these foundries and confound our foes.

OBI-WAN   Thine instincts serve thee well, young Padawan.
             I prithee let us fly and make attack   15
             Upon the Federation starships, quick!

PADMÉ   O, how the battle rages down below!
             The battle droids array'd both small and large,
             With droidekas beside them in the fight.
             Behold how they assault with armor'd tanks,   20

Contraptions spinning with enormous wheels,
Swift flying drones that soar toward their marks,
With missiles, lasers, blasters, which illume
The sky. See lights of blue and red twixt us
And them, an 'twere a pyrotechnic show.   25
Yet still the troopers on our side strive on,
Destroying one of their vast starships, look—
A sandstorm furious it doth create!
Our dauntless troopers move into the fray,
O'ercoming all the droids by higher sums: 30
The battle, which doth seem a clash betwixt
Two massive armies, equal in their strength,
Belike 'tis, finally, a numbers game.

They continue to fly. Enter COUNT DOOKU, NUTE GUNRAY, POGGLE
THE LESSER, *and other* GEONOSIANS *in the command center.*

NUTE   The Jedi have amass'd an army vast!
DOOKU   That seemeth most impossible, for how   35
             Could they a force so quickly generate?
NUTE   With ev'ry droid available we'll strike.
DOOKU   There are too many troops against us here.
POGGLE   Besides, communications have been block'd.
NUTE   This situation bodes not well for us—   40
             The starships must return to space anon.
                                              [Exit Nute.

POGGLE   Our only option now is to retreat.
DOOKU   My master strong shall never tolerate
             Republic and its treachery herein.
POGGLE   Death doth await us here if we do stay.   45
             E'en more, we shall lose something even more:

All warriors shall flee to th'catacombs.
Thus shall the Jedi never find the thing
Hid shrewdly here on Geonosis, yea—
Safeguarded plans for weapon ultimate   50
That shall th'Republic shatter once complete.
Aye, were they to discover these designs,
Receive a traitor's doom we surely would.

DOOKU   You may entrust me with those sly designs;
I shall take them along to Coruscant.   55
In safety with my master they'll reside.
Now, let us ride and join the battle, comrades!

                    [Count Dooku and two Geonosians board
                        speeder bikes and fly from the command center.
                    Exeunt Poggle the Lesser and other Geonosians.

OBI-WAN   Observe below!
ANAKIN   —'Tis Dooku! Shoot him down.
TROOPER 3   The rockets all are spent.
ANAKIN   —Then follow on!
PADMÉ   The man is full of might and fury, too: 60
We shall need help to overcome his pow'r.
OBI-WAN   Yet neither time nor help we have enough:
If we do wait for help, the time is past.
I'll warrant Anakin and I can stop
Count Dooku—we are ample time and help.   65
DOOKU   I sense 'tis Jedi who do trail me now.
Companions, fall behind whilst they give chase.

                    [The Geonosians fall away from Dooku and
                        take position on the other side of the balcony.

ANAKIN   Alas, now come the blasts behind us, fie!
Our ship is harshly struck!
PADMÉ   —I fall once more!

                    [Padmé and Clone Trooper 4 fall from the balcony

                    onto the sand of Geonosis. Exeunt Count Dooku
                           and Geonosians into a tower hangar.

ANAKIN   Nay—Padmé! Prithee, land this ship anon!   70

OBI-WAN   Let not thy feelings personal betray
                Our mission, Anakin. [*To trooper pilot:*] The speeder still
                Pursue, for 'tis our one and only aim.

ANAKIN   Nay, lower down the ship.

OBI-WAN   —I'll ne'er defeat
                Count Dooku by myself, for he is skill'd   75
                With some dark, unimaginable strength!
                I need thee, Anakin: if we can catch
                The man, belike this war shall quickly end.
                We have employment most essential, which
                Doth supersede thy private interests!   80

ANAKIN   I care not for your mission or your war—
                'Tis Padmé who doth stir mine only thoughts.
                The ship must land!

OBI-WAN   —Thou shalt excluded be
                From our strong Jedi Order. Car'st thou not?

ANAKIN   I cannot leave my love in such a state.   85

OBI-WAN   Speak thou with sense: let reason fill thy mind.
                How dost thou think thy Padmé would comport
                Herself, if she were fac'd with such a choice?

ANAKIN   She would her duty serve in ev'ry thing.

OBI-WAN   Thus thou shalt too, and so we hurry on—   90
                Toward the tower whither Dooku fled!

                [*Exeunt Obi-Wan, Anakin, and Clone Trooper 3.*

        Enter YODA *below, aside with* CLONE TROOPER 1.

YODA   Such tension sense I,

Betwixt Obi-Wan and his
Brave young Anakin.

TROOPER 1   The army of the droids doth make retreat.   95
YODA   Well done, Commander.
              Bring me a ship, that I may
              Make pursuit anon.

                                        [Exit Clone Trooper 1.

              This feeling shaketh
              E'en to my very spirit: 100
              Not well it bodeth.

                                        [Exit Yoda.

TROOPER 4   Dear lady, are you injur'd?
PADMÉ   —Nay, sirrah.
TROOPER 4   With all due haste we should make way unto
              The forward center of command, e'en now.
PADMÉ   Nay, hear thou my command, brave trooper: we   105
              Shall go unto the hangar in a trice.
              I prithee, find a transport we may use!
TROOPER 4   'Tis done, my lady, e'en as you command it.

                                        [Exit Clone Trooper 4.

PADMÉ   Mine Anakin, my love, did leave me here,
              Ne'er knowing what web Fate had spun for me.   110
              Was this some oversight of love most blind,
              Or did he, in the instant, choose some path
              That led him hence, e'en from his fallen love?
              Nay, I'd not have it so: the man is true.
              We must not let our passion override   115
              Our sense, which knoweth that to which 'tis call'd.
              Belike his duty did inform his acts,
              Responsibility his movements urg'd.
              Do not mistrust thine heart's own second half,

O, Padmé: he is truer far beyond   120
Thyself, for thou dost doubt whilst he doth serve.
Be still, then, fear, and rally to his cause:
Sweet Anakin, I come unto thine aid,
Ne'ermore to doubt the love thou hast display'd.

                                        [Exit Padmé.

SCENE 3.

On the planet Geonosis in the tower hangar.

Enter COUNT DOOKU.

DOOKU   The army of the clones hath been reveal'd
           Far sooner than my master did design,
           Yet it shall be of little consequence.
           His plan is perfectly constructed, not
           To be disrupted by such accidents.   5
           The Jedi make pursuit, and shall anon
           Be here. I greet the fight to come with glee,
           For they shall witness power far beyond
           Their expectation and their knowledge, yea.
           This day the dark side of the Force shall be   10
           Made plain for all to see, and Obi-Wan—
           So saturated with a Jedi's pride—
           And his naïve, young, sniv'ling Padawan
           Shall know the dread that from the dark side comes.
           What joy, to have a potent hand in this,   15
           What bliss, this frightful faculty to wield,
           What ecstasy, my master's will to serve,
           What pleasure, to unveil his awful might.

The Jedi come and soon the Jedi pass,
And thus the Sith shall dominate the scene.   20

Enter OBI-WAN KENOBI *and* ANAKIN SKYWALKER.

ANAKIN   You shall make ample recompense for all
            Those Jedi whom you slaughter'd here today.
OBI-WAN   Let us take him together, Anakin.
            Proceed thou left—
ANAKIN   —Nay, I shall take him now!
OBI-WAN   O, quick, impulsive rush of reckless youth!   25
DOOKU   If thou wouldst move as swift as lightning, boy,
            Thou dost a taste of lightning's touch deserve.
                    [Count Dooku strikes Anakin with lightning
                              from his hands, felling him.
            You see, bold Obi-Wan, my Jedi pow'rs
            Are greater far than yours: surrender, then.
OBI-WAN   It shall not be. Your lightning doth impress,   30
            Yet I believe your thunder is but noise.
                                        [They duel.
DOOKU   Rash Master Obi-Wan, you disappoint:
            Your strength is weak, though Yoda doth place you
            In such a high esteem. Have you no more?
            Can you not best an old man as myself?   35
OBI-WAN   [*aside:*] What gift of darkness here he doth display—
            Such terrible and wondrous vigor. Fie!
            The man is far more powerful than I.
DOOKU   Feel now the wrath of my lightsaber's sting.
                    [Count Dooku hits Obi-Wan on the arm
                        and leg with his lightsaber, cutting him.
                              Obi-Wan falls to the ground.

         This final blow doth end you, Obi-Wan.   40

ANAKIN   Yet not whilst I have life or breath to move!
         If you would slay my master, you should know
         I stand athwart the passage thither, rogue,
         And you must make your wicked way past me.
             [Anakin jumps in and blocks Dooku's lightsaber
                 as Dooku prepares to slay Obi-Wan.

DOOKU   'Tis brave, young one, yet I would think thou hadst   45
         Thy lesson learn'd. Shall I school thee again?

ANAKIN   For certain I am but a pupil slow
         To learn, especially from teachers vile.

OBI-WAN   Good Anakin—take thou my lightsaber!
         Mine arms may not assist thee, so take thou   50
         Their natural extension, Padawan!
             [Obi-Wan throws his lightsaber to Anakin,
                 who begins dueling Count Dooku with a
                 lightsaber in each hand.

DOOKU   This double threat is merely double chance,
         And twice the opportunity for me.
         Yet feel my blast, and double now is single!
         Thy lightsaber in twain, upon my stroke.   55
             [Dooku cuts one of Anakin's lightsabers
                 in two. They continue to duel.

ANAKIN   A single death shall be enough for you!

DOOKU   [aside:] The boy hath might—the Force is strong with him,
         Indeed he doth begin to wear on me,
         Yet I shall conquer him with greater vigor.
         I shall not strike him down, but teach to him   60
         A lesson that he shall not soon forget.
            [Count Dooku uses his lightsaber to cut off Anakin's
               arm and throw him backward, near Obi-Wan.

ANAKIN   Alack! Mine arm, cut off before its time—
              O, cruelty, O, bitter agony!
              Pray, Master, do forgive, I am unarm'd
              And have no tool with which to make defense.   65
              Pray, Master, do forgive, I am disarm'd,
              And cannot fight to save you or myself.
              How shall I hold my Padmé's hand in mine,
              How shall I stroke her hair of softest strands,
              How shall I feel the smoothness in her cheek,   70
              How shall I wrap her in a fond embrace?
              O, arm, mine instrument of youthful love,
              How shall I woo without thee by my side?
DOOKU   The battle now is done, and I may flee.

                        Enter YODA.

              Old Master Yoda, have you come as well?   75
              Shall you, like these two frail and fractur'd men,
              Have your days number'd by the crafty count?
              Your Jedi Order weak hath interfer'd
              In our affairs but one too many times.
              The sum is this: we shall your ranks divide   80
              And multiply your suffering sans end.
                    [*Count Dooku uses the Force to break off pieces
                    of the hangar, sending them hurling toward Yoda.
                            Yoda uses the Force to hold them at bay.*
YODA   Indeed, 'tis certain:
              Powerful you are, Dooku.
              The dark side I sense.

              Yet your figures fail—   85
              All adds not up as you see—

For the Force mine is.

Your equation's wrong,
For integral the Force is:
On this you may count.   90

DOOKU   I calculate my powers rise above
The quantity in any Jedi Knight.
Naught in the galaxy shall e'er subtract
My strength, which runs toward infinity.
E'en you cannot withstand my total pow'r.   95

       [Count Dooku releases lightning from his
              hands, which Yoda deflects.

YODA   Much to learn you have,
Your dark shall ne'er outnumber
Mine arithmetic.

DOOKU   'Tis obvious this fight shall not be won
By tallying our knowledge of the Force,   100

But by some other calculus, indeed.
Lightsabers may test our equality,
Then shall we see who's greater and who's less.
                              [*Yoda and Count Dooku duel.*

YODA   I skip and parry,
              Soar as I have for e'en more   105
              Than eight hundred years.

DOOKU   [*aside:*] His speed: how unexpected and profound!
              His skill: beyond the measure of a man!
              His energy: near inconceivable!
              His grace: how like an angel doth he fly!   110
              I cannot win this contest, now I know—
              Though I with all my dark arts skillful am,
              It seems he is of dark and light combin'd,
              The owner of the rainbow's very glow,
              With wisdom far surpassing all the world.   115

YODA   Fought ably you have,
              Former Padawan of mine,
              Yet I am Master.

DOOKU   This is but the beginning, Yoda, aye—
              Your love of others shall be your undoing!   120
                    [*Count Dooku uses the Force to knock one of the
                        hangar's columns onto Obi-Wan and Anakin.*

OBI-WAN   Alas, this is the end—the rocks and things
              That Dooku threw toward him once before
              Are nothing next to this vast pillar. O,
              My spirit, be prepar'd to meet thy death!

YODA   Enormous it is   125
              Only if with eyes I look;
              The Force better sees.
                    [*Exit Count Dooku as Yoda uses the Force
                        to catch the column and throw it aside.*

OBI-WAN   Immense authority in one so small,
               I ne'er would have believ'd it possible.
               My life he spares to live another day—   130
               He shall not yet see Obi-Wan as ghost.
YODA   [*aside:*] Now worse matters are,
               This grim pow'r a threat portends:
               Dark from dark shall come.

          Enter PADMÉ *with a battalion of* CLONE TROOPERS.

PADMÉ   O, Anakin, how art thou sore abus'd!   135
ANAKIN   My Padmé sweet, thou art alive and well,
               And I am thine, though by the dark side us'd.
PADMÉ   Together we shall journey through this hell.
OBI-WAN   [*aside to Yoda:*] These protestations of affection ring
               Most dissonantly on mine ears, and yet   140
               They hold no great surprise. Mayhap we were
               Unwise to let these two become so close.
YODA   'Tis he must decide—
               His love or the Jedi path—
               A choice he now hath.   145

                                                        [*Exeunt.*

SCENE 4.

On the planet Coruscant.

          Enter DARTH SIDIOUS *and* COUNT DOOKU *on balcony.*

DOOKU   The Force is with us, Master Sidious.
SIDIOUS   I welcome thee with joy, brave Lord Tyranus.

                    You have serv'd well in ev'ry matter and
                    Deserve thy master's commendation rich.
DOOKU   'Tis privilege to serve, Darth Sidious.
                    Moreover, Master, I share this report:
                    The war begins, which we two did design.
SIDIOUS   Most excellent, astute apprentice mine.
                    All doth proceed exactly as I've plann'd.

                                                    [Exeunt.

              Enter YODA, MACE WINDU, *and* OBI-WAN KENOBI
                          in the Jedi temple.

OBI-WAN   Brave masters both, think ye it may be true—   1
                    What Dooku said of Sidious' complete
                    Control o'er all the Senate? Can it be?
YODA   Join'd with the dark side
                    Count Dooku hath, verily.
                    Certain that much is.   1

                    Lying, deceiving,
                    Scheming, fomenting mistrust:
                    These are now his ways.
MACE   'Tis possible his words no cleaner than
                    The dung of bantha are—yet still methinks   2
                    Perforce the Senate must be closer watch'd.
YODA   Yea, Master Windu,
                    Mine opinion and your own
                    One and the same are.
MACE   Where is your keen apprentice, Anakin—   2
                    Hath he been plung'd into a sea of love?

OBI-WAN   He hath escorted Amidala home,
            Back to the planet of Naboo they go.
            What there his actions are, I cannot say.
            But, sir, about this recent battle I   30
            Have thought at length: without the clones it were
            Republic loss, and not a victory.
YODA   "Victory," say you?
            'Tis no noble victory,
            Master Obi-Wan.   35

            The dark side's curtain
            Falls gloomily o'er our play;
            The Clone War begins.
                 [Obi-Wan comes forward as the others freeze.

        Enter ANAKIN SKYWALKER and PADMÉ on balcony.

ANAKIN   New fear o'er the Republic settles fast,
            As by our enemies we are disarm'd.   40
            Deceit and cunning fall on ev'ry side,
            And rumor of an unknown threat doth grow.
PADMÉ   Along the way, some learn'd to speak in love,
            And others learn'd the cost of arrogance.
            Some teachers found that they had much to learn,   45
            Whilst learners overtook their masters true.
OBI-WAN   Disruption and mistrust do grow as weeds,
            A bitter atmosphere for the Republic.
            The star wars we must wage begin—'tis clear—
            As all our certainty doth turn to fear.   50

              Enter CHORUS as epilogue.

CHORUS   Our play doth end upon a fretful note,
As worry o'er the dark side doth pervade:
The evil Sith their wicked plans promote
Whilst Yoda and Mace Windu are dismay'd.
The clones in their battalions are a sight:
Their hundreds and their thousands fall in line.
Against the legions of the droids they'll fight;
The galaxy in conflict they entwine.
Upon Naboo, a hopeful final scene,
With Padmé married to her Anakin.
His arm hath been restor'd, though 'tis machine,
Their love doth bloom while war comes creeping in.
There, worthy friends, our drama ends forthwith,
Before revenge is taken by the Sith.

[Exeunt omnes.

END.

AFTERWORD.

Two classic theatrical devices seem tailor made for this adaptation of *Attack of the Clones*, with its knotty twists of who's good and who's bad, who knows what and who doesn't, and who trusts and doesn't trust whom. The first is Rumor, whom I borrowed from Shakespeare's *Henry IV, Part 2* for use in *William Shakespeare's The Phantom of Menace*. Rumor's job is to build confusion and mistrust, which is perfect for this tale, in which confusion and mistrust are the order of the day. Second, we have the ancient Greek character of the Moirai, which translates into English as the Fates. They appear regularly through *William Shakespeare's The Clone Army Attacketh*, though I've condensed them to a single Fate. The Fates, of course, spin threads of destiny for each of us. They can turn anyone's thread into a complex web, or cut the thread short at any moment. This notion resonates perfectly with *Attack of the Clones*, which weaves webs of plot as complex as any the Fates ever spun.

The relationship between Padmé and Anakin is central to the prequels, and a key piece of that relationship is Padmé's transition from thinking of Anakin as a boy to seeing him as a man and, finally, as a lover. My hope was to make their wooing believable and romantic, and to that end I made three decisions. First, the interactions during which Padmé and Anakin fall in love—which occur across a few separate scenes in *Attack of the Clones*—become a single, longer scene in *William Shakespeare's The Clone Army Attacketh*. Specifically, Act III, scene 1, a central section of the story. Second, I wanted the strength of Shakespeare's romantic plotlines to surround and embrace Padmé and Anakin. That large scene, therefore, includes lines spoken by characters from each of Shakespeare's comedies—and, for good measure, *Romeo and Juliet*. Finally, once the stage directions indicate that Padmé and Anakin touch for the first time, the two speak together in rhyming quatrains—four lines with an ABAB rhyme scheme—as did Romeo and Juliet. (I gave Han and Leia the same rhyming pattern in *The Empire Striketh Back* and *The Jedi Doth Return*. But Padmé and Anakin are alone with each other much more often than Han and Leia are, so their lines rhyme far more frequently.)

As this series progresses, I am having more and more fun playing with language, hiding things here and there, just having a big ol' geeky time. In *The Clone Army Attacketh*, two word games are based on the idea of cloning. First, Jango Fett speaks in prose, as does his son Boba Fett in the original *William Shakespeare's Star Wars* trilogy. And, just for kicks, each of Jango's sentences begins and ends with the same letter. Why? He is the prototype of all the clones, so the first letter of the sentence is cloned at the end. (This is also the case when any clone troopers speak, though they speak in iambic pentameter.) Second, for the cloners on Kamino I wanted to do something extra special. The memorable characters Lama Su and Taun We appear in only one long scene—split into a few shots—in *Attack of the Clones*. For their scene here, I took a page from Douglas Hofstadter, author of the book *Gödel, Escher, Bach*, and his palindromelike "Crab Canon" dialogue. The structure of the cloners' dialogue uniquely shows off their ability to clone: each line of iambic pentameter they speak is repeated later, in reverse, so that their lines follow an ABCDEDCBA structure. (Only the punctuation changes.) The center of their speech is Lama Su's lengthy explanation of the clones and the process of making them. After that, Lama Su's and Taun We's lines begin repeating, in the opposite order in which we first heard them. Following in this structure was tricky, but it brought deep satisfaction to my inner nerd.

Other character tidbits to look for: Dexter Jettster, the four-armed proprietor of Dex's Diner, uses some sort of arm, hand, or finger imagery in every line he speaks, a little nod to the fact that he has more arms than the rest of us (and is therefore dexterous!). When C-3PO's body is put on a battle droid head and his head is attached to a battle droid body, he becomes C-3PO 1 and C-3PO 2, respectively. The three beasts in the execution arena on Geonosis—the reek, the acklay, and the nexu—take after Macbeth's three witches, complete with rhyming couplets and iambic tetrameter.

I hope you find as much geeky fun reading *William Shakespeare's The Clone Army Attacketh* as I had putting geeky fun into it. If so, we might (geekily) say my fun has been cloned in you, dear reader.

ACKNOWLEDGMENTS.

This book was written while my family and I spent time on North Ronaldsay, the northernmost of Scotland's Orkney Islands. Thank you to everyone on the island for the gift of hospitality, particularly our hosts, Helga and Michael Scott and baby Isabella, and Jimmy Craigie, who kept us moving.

Thanks to my parents, Beth and Bob Doescher, my brother Erik and his family Em, Aracelli, and Addison, and my aunt Holly Havens. Thank you, always, to Josh Hicks and to Murray Biggs.

Thank you to the wonderful people of Quirk Books: Jason Rekulak, Rick Chillot, Nicole De Jackmo, Suzanne Wallace, Eric Smith, Brett Cohen, Jane Morley, Tim O'Donnell, and everyone else at Quirk. This is book number five with Quirk, and they manage to keep it fun. Thank you to my agent, Adriann Ranta, for Yoda-like guidance and support. Thank you to Jennifer Heddle at Lucasfilm for making this an enjoyable process and to illustrator Nicolas Delort for making the books shine.

Thank you to the people whom I always thank, because they are always wonderful: Heidi Altman and Scott Roehm, Emmy Betz and Michael Hoke, Jane Bidwell, Travis Boeh and Sarah Woodburn, Chris Buehler and Marian Hammond, Erin and Nathan Buehler, Jeff and Caryl Creswell, Ken Evers-Hood, Mark Fordice, Chris Frimoth, Alana Garrigues, Brian Heron, Jim and Nancy Hicks, Anne Huebsch, Apricot and David Irving, Doree Jarboe, Alexis Kaushansky, Bobby Lopez, Chris and Andrea Martin, Jessica Mason, Bruce McDonald, Joan and Grady Miller, Jim Moiso, Janice Morgan, Michael Morrill and Tara Schuster, Dave Nieuwstraten, Omid Nooshin, Bill Rauch, Julia Rodriguez-O'Donnell, Larry Rothe, Kristy Thompson, Naomi Walcott and Audu Besmer, Steve Weeks, Ryan Wilmot, Ben and Katie Wire, Ethan Youngerman and Rebecca Lessem, Dan Zehr, and members of the 501st Legion.

To my spouse, Jennifer, and our children, Liam and Graham: thank you. I love you three dearly, and if I could clone you . . . well, I wouldn't. Because that would just be weird.

MAY
THE VERSE
BE WITH
YOU!

WILLIAM SHAKESPEARE'S STAR WARS TRILOGY
THE ROYAL IMPERIAL BOXED SET
Includes episodes 4–6 plus an exclusive full-color poster

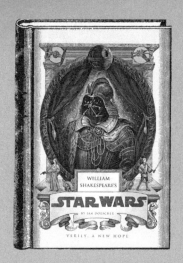

William Shakespeare's
Star Wars: Verily, A New Hope

COLLECT THE

William Shakespeare's
The Empire Striketh Back

William Shakespeare's
The Jedi Doth Return

William Shakespeare's
The Phantom of Menace

ENTIRE SAGA!

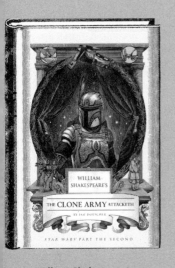

William Shakespeare's
The Clone Army Attacketh

COMING

SEPTEMBER

2015!

William Shakespeare's
Tragedy of the Sith's Revenge

SONNET 2.0
"Shall I Compare Thee to HTML?"

The Clone Wars are with clamor now begun,
Whilst Anakin and Padmé flee for love.
Let brutal war unto its warring run,
And lovers rest with song of lark and dove.
Our play hath ended, over far too soon,
Yet pleasures for the soul await online!
No more allow thy heart to cry and swoon,
But get thee quick unto computer thine!
The Quirk Books site hath wonders still for thee:
An **interview** with author Ian Doescher,
An **educators' guide** is thine for free,
And our most **bookish blog** hath ne'er been fresher.
Fly to QuirkBooks-dot-com, be not postpon'd—
And may the mirth thou foundest here be clon'd!

quirkbooks.com/theclonearmyattacketh